MW01625498

Crying Freeman

Shades of Death

Part 3

VIZ GRAPHIC NOVEL

SHADES *of* DEATH

Crying Freeman Graphic Novel

Part 3

STORY BY

KAZUO KOIKE

ART BY

RYOICHI IKEGAMI

CONTENTS

Chapter 5	The Killing Ring	Part 6	7
		Part 7	25
		Part 8	45
Chapter 6	Sister	Part 1	63
		Part 2	81
		Part 3	99
		Part 4	117
		Part 5	135
		Part 6	155
		Part 7	173

Story by Kazuo Koike
Art by Ryoichi Ikegami
★
English Adaptation/Will Jacobs
Touch Up Art & Lettering/Wayne Truman
Cover Design/Viz Graphics
Executive Editor/Seiji Horibuchi
Editor/Satoru Fujii
★
First Published by Shogakukan, Inc., in Japan
Editor-in-Chief/Yonosuke Konishi
Executive Editor/Katsuya Shirai
★

★
Published by Viz Communications, Inc.
P.O. Box 77010, San Francisco, CA 94107.
★
10 9 8 7 6 5 4 3 2 1
First Printing May 1992

Chapter 5

The Killing Ring Part 6

SCREEEE

EEYOO EEYOO
EEYOO
CK 426
DENTS ESC
CK 426
DENTS ESC

TP TP TP TP
CK 426
EIDENTS ESCORT

OHHHHHH

RMMMMM

TRRRRRT

RMMMMM

SCREEE

ALERT THE SOLDIERS, MILANDA. I'LL GO CHECK THE SCENE.
I CAN'T BELIEVE THAT SHIKEBARO IS DEAD...

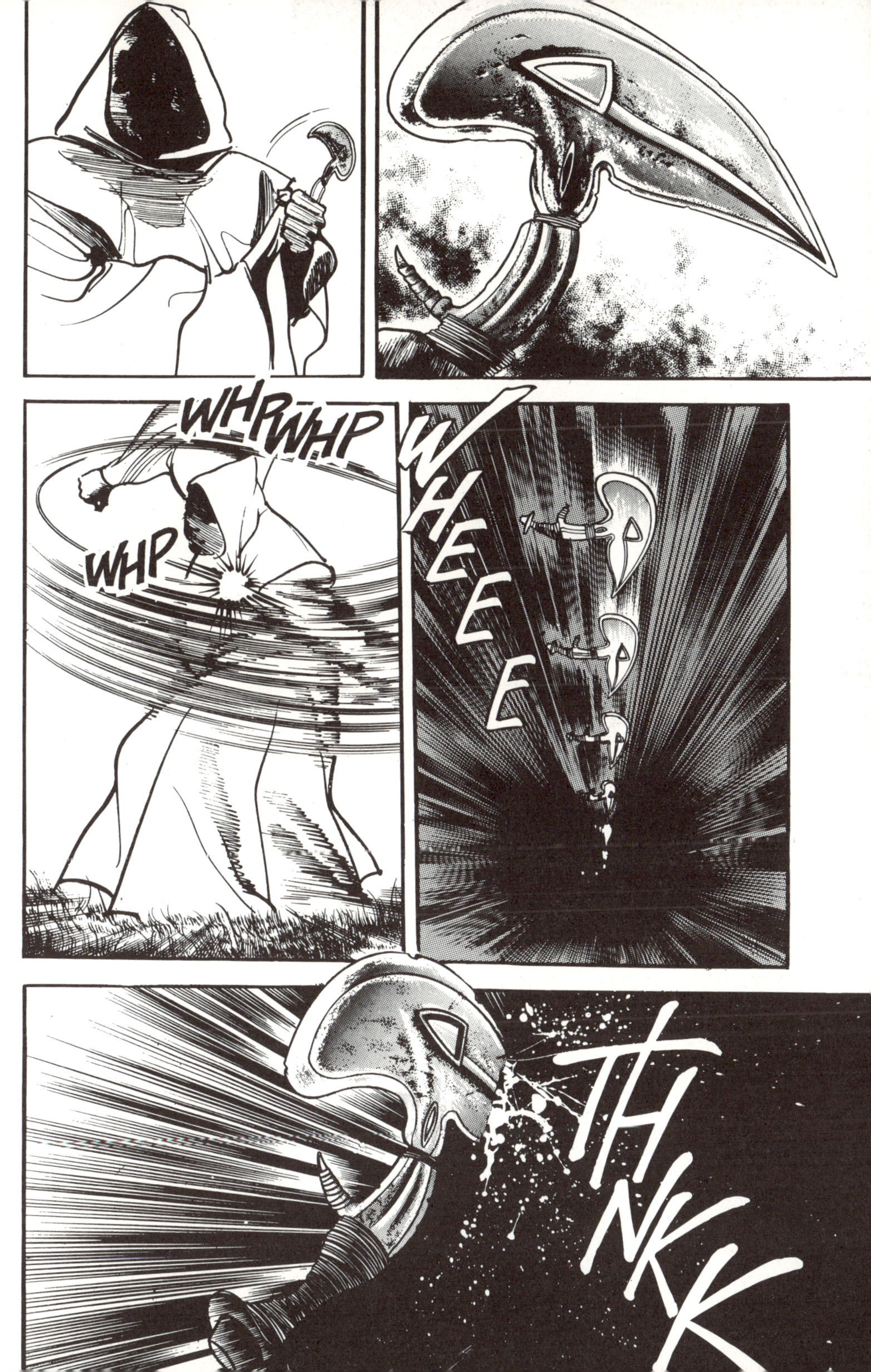
WHPWHP
WHP
WHEEEE
THNKK

HIIII
FPPR
WHEEE

AGHHH

HOW DARE YOU...
HOW DARE YOU BRING DEATH TO ME...?

THNKKK
MI... MILANDA...
SLGHH
WHPP
AGGGHH

UGH

SLSHH

UGHHHH

IT'S OVER...
THE ASKARI ORGANIZATION WILL FALL APART NOW.
KREEEK
WHEEE

WHEEE
AHHHH

UHH

I AM BUGNUG.
I AM THE TRUE LEADER OF THE ASKARI.

DAMN.
I WAS CARELESS...
JIGON WAS NOT THE LAST IN THE CHAIN OF COMMAND.
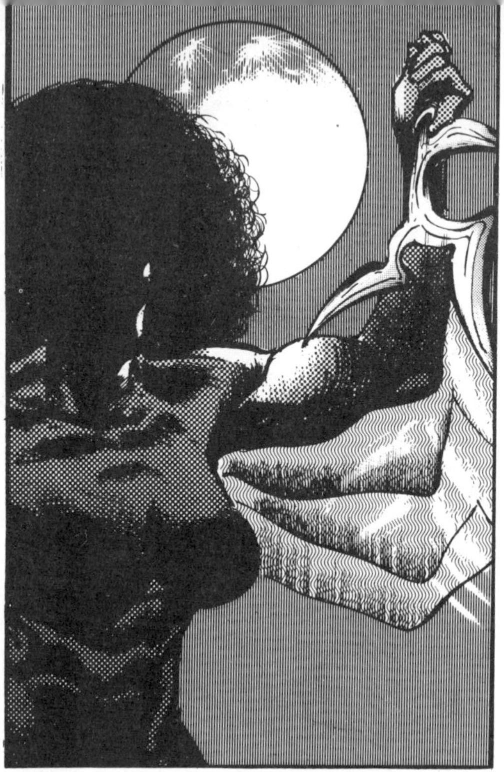

YOU MUST BE FREEMAN, YES?

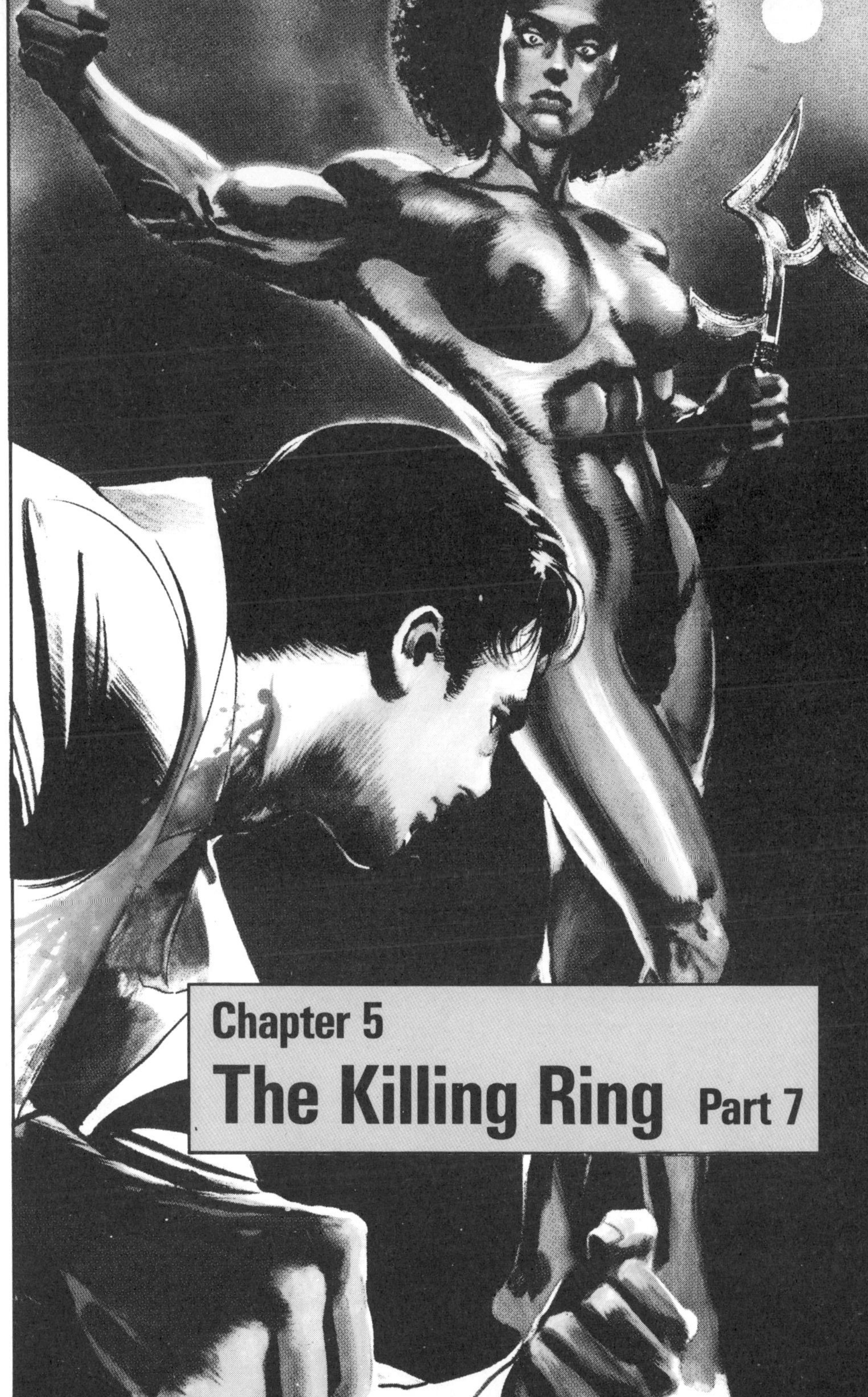
Chapter 5
The Killing Ring Part 7

HIII
YAA
WHIP

WHPP
KLNKK

WOOSH

FPPP

HSSSS

KLNKK

WHPP

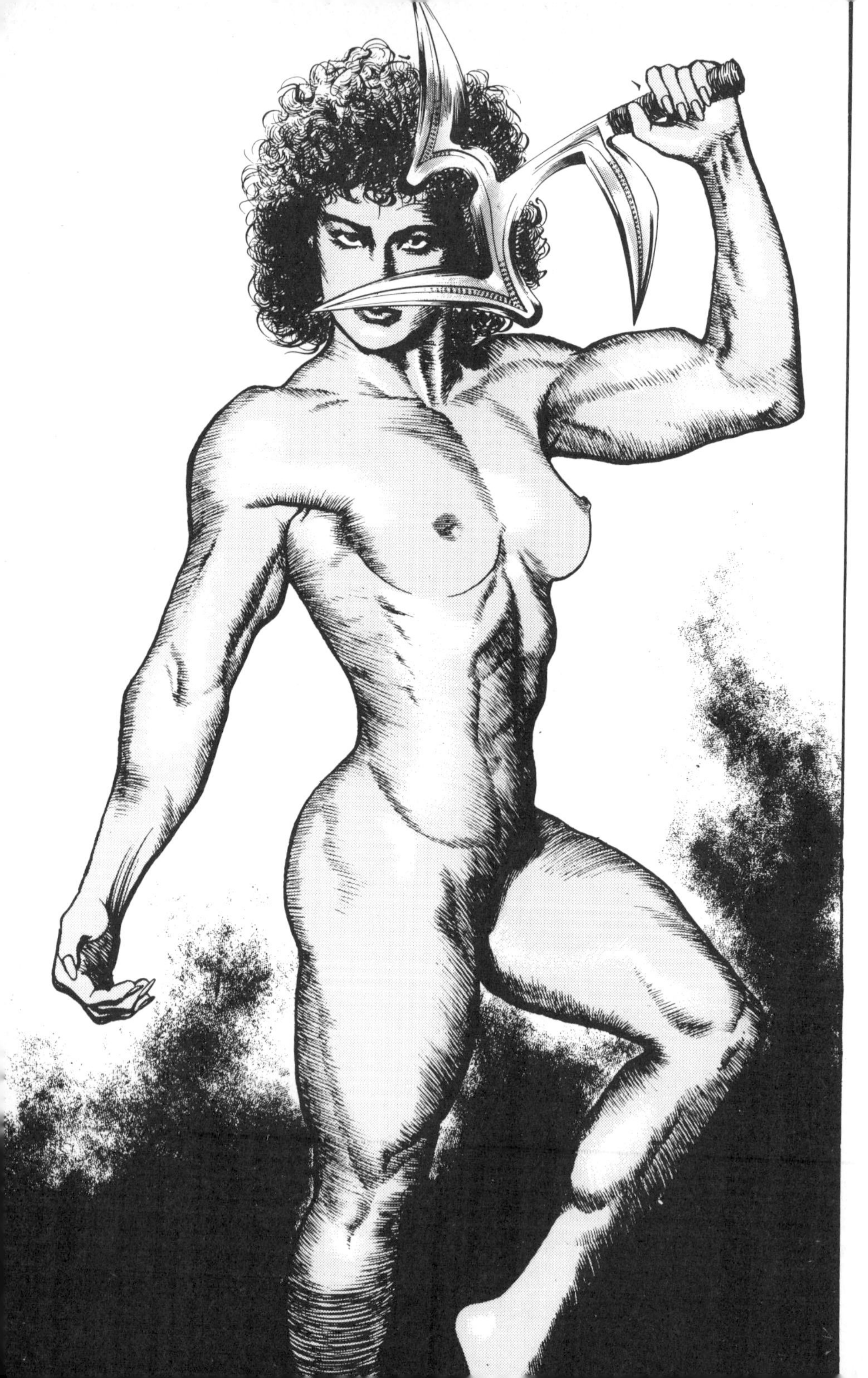

HOOO
WHPP
WHEE
KLNKK
WHMPP
SNP
SNP

BEAUTIFUL. IT IS SAID THAT ONE WHO DRINKS THE BLOOD OF THE DRAGON GAINS ETERNAL LIFE.

WHP
WHP
WHP

WHP
WHP WHP
TP

WHSH!

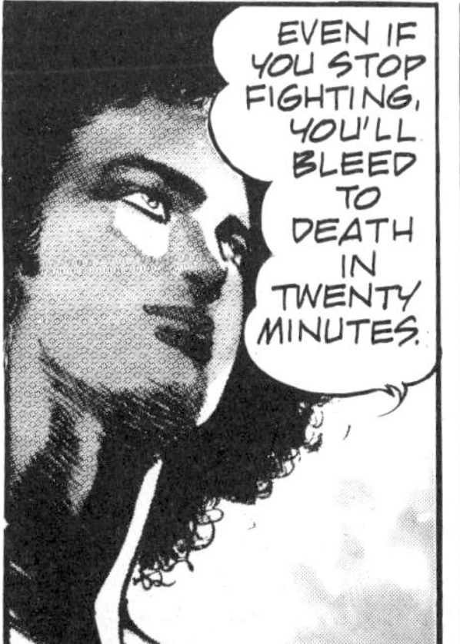
EVEN IF YOU STOP FIGHTING, YOU'LL BLEED TO DEATH IN TWENTY MINUTES.

BUT I INTEND TO PUT YOUR BLOOD TO BETTER USE.

THNKK
AIIII
WMPPP

TWPPP

WHSHH

WHSHH

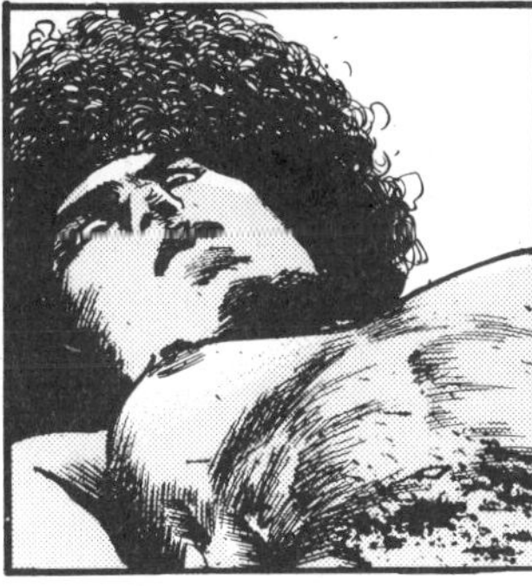

WHOOO

WHSHH

WP WP WP
WP
WP

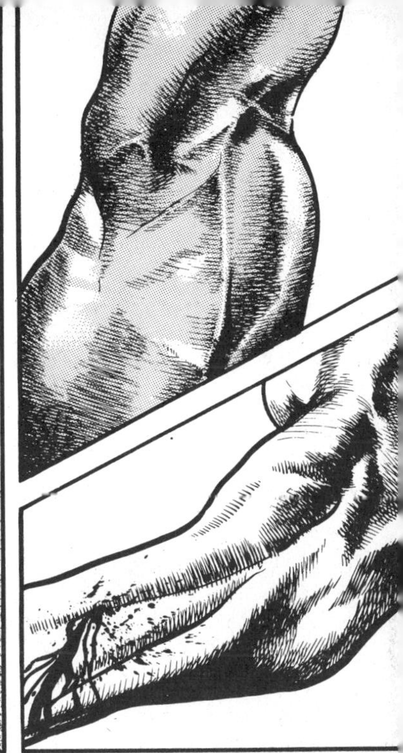

ARGHHH

UGGH

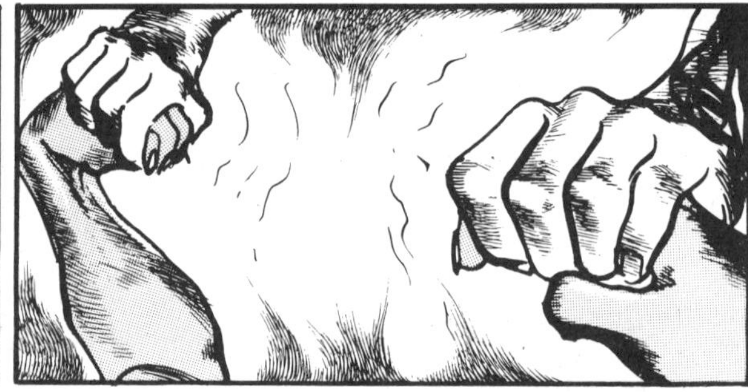

ugggggh

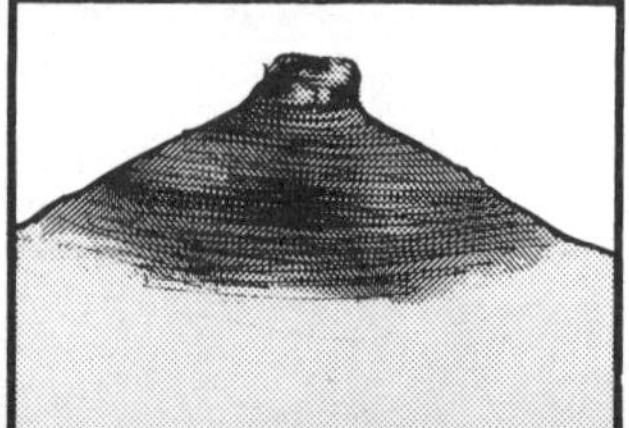

I'LL BITE IT OFF!
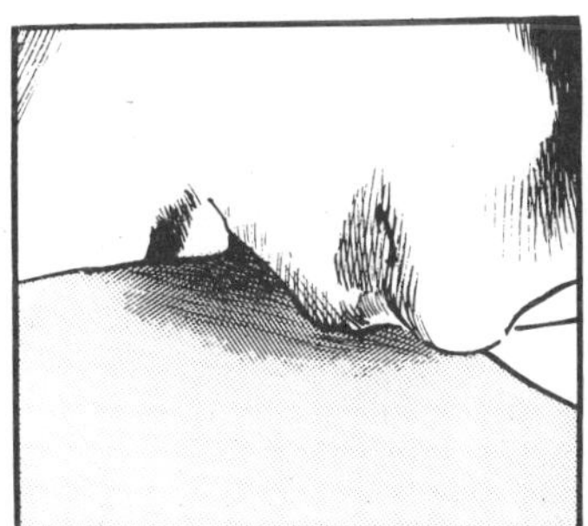

AHHHH

OHHHHH

Yaaaaaa

UGNN

PLP
PLP

MM
MM
MM
GLB
GLB

HMM
MM

BUGNUG. WHAT DOES THE NAME MEAN ?

ANTEATER.

AN ANTEATER THAT SWALLOWED MY BLOOD! Ha Ha Ha Ha Ha!

WHOOOSH

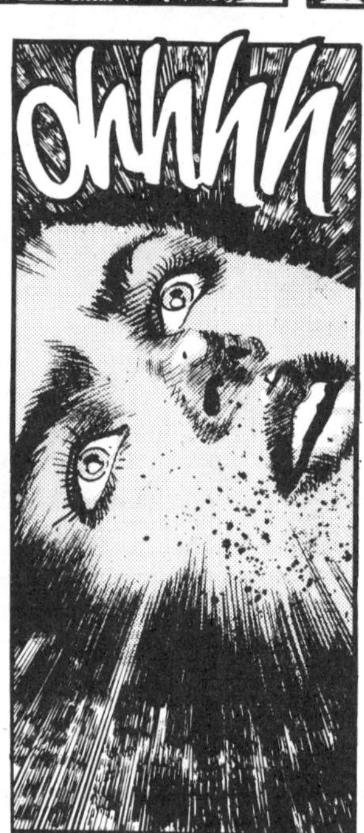
ohhhh

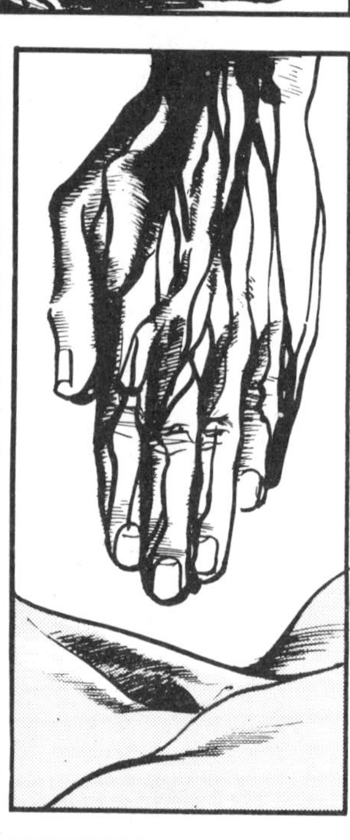

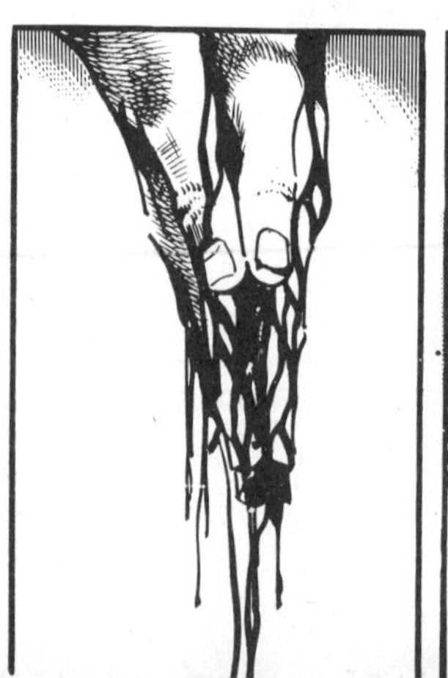

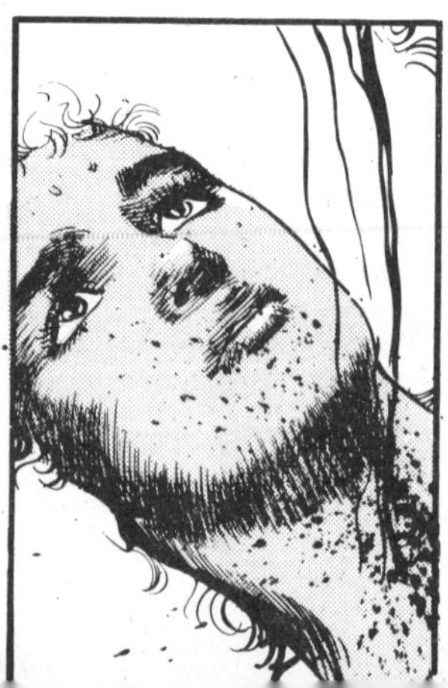

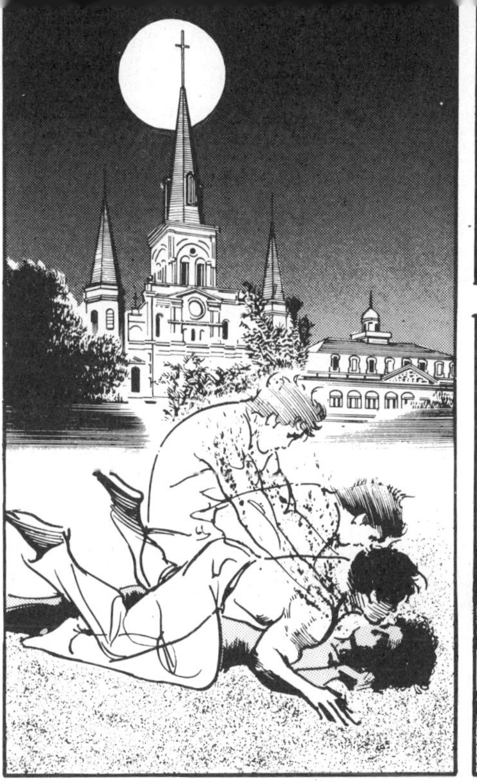

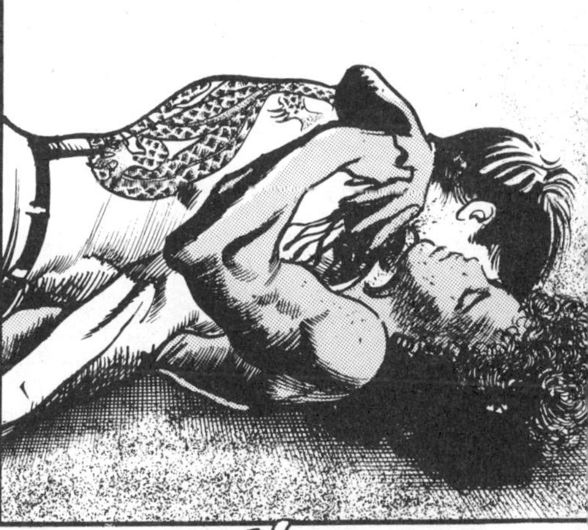

WHAT A MAN! SO CONFIDENT! SO SURE THAT HE COULD BEND ME TO HIS WILL!
HE COULD HAVE MUTILATED ME. HE COULD HAVE KILLED ME, BUT HE DIDN'T.

HMMM

IF HE HAD WANTED TO KILL ME, HE WOULD HAVE. WHY DID HE DISPLAY SUCH MERCY?

WAS HE INTIMATING THAT WE SHOULD STOP THIS FIGHTING?
ONE THING IS FOR CERTAIN. BOTH THE 108 DRAGONS AND THE ASKARI HAVE ALREADY SHED TOO MUCH BLOOD, SACRIFICED TOO MANY LIVES.

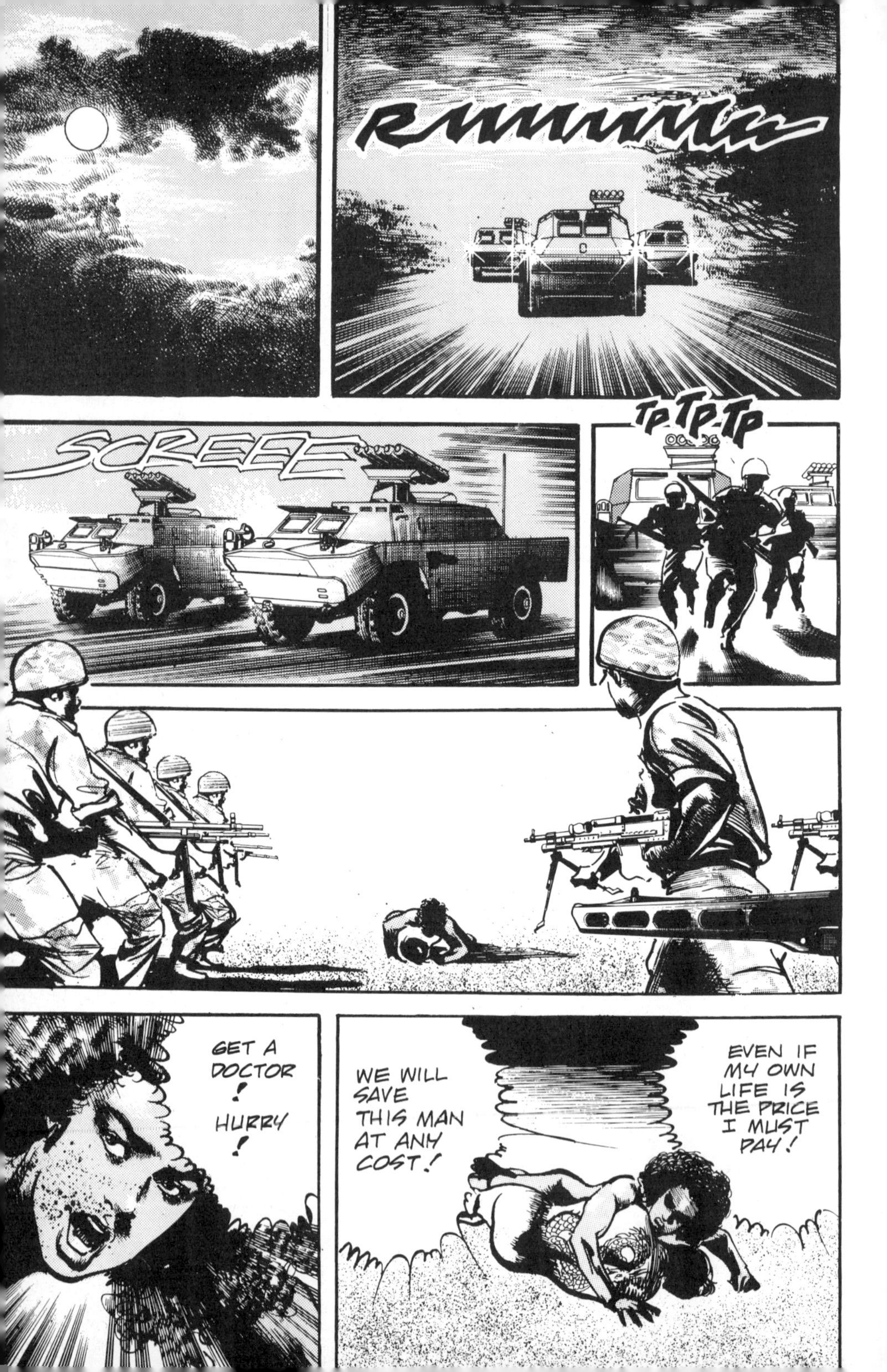

SCREEE

TP-TP-TP

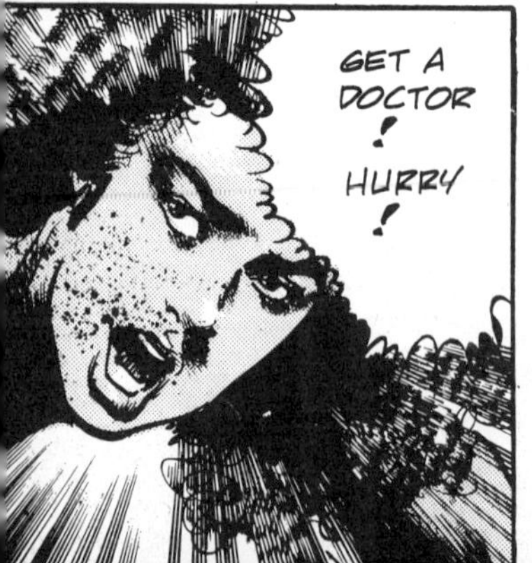

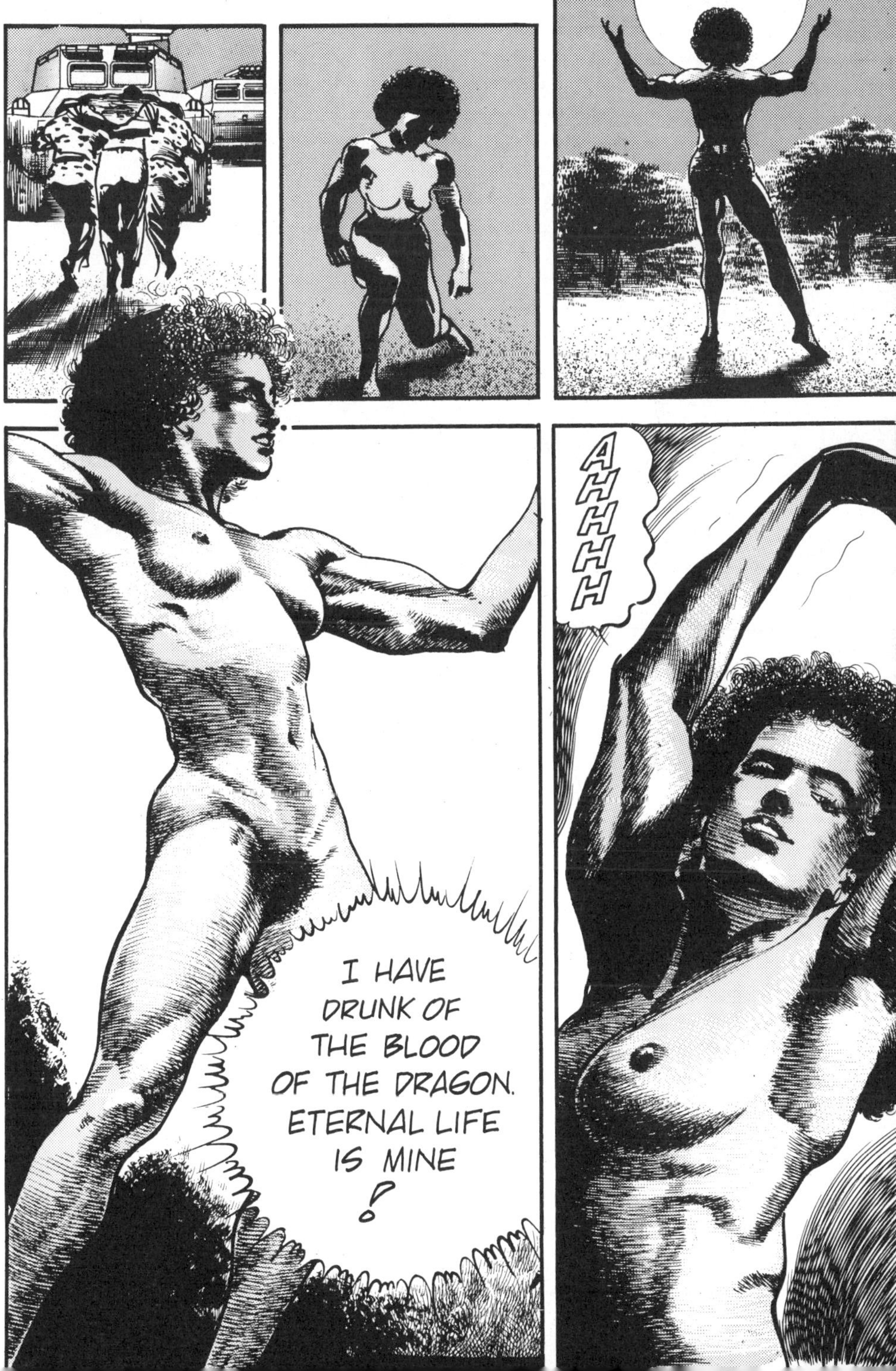
I HAVE DRUNK OF THE BLOOD OF THE DRAGON. ETERNAL LIFE IS MINE !
AHHHHH

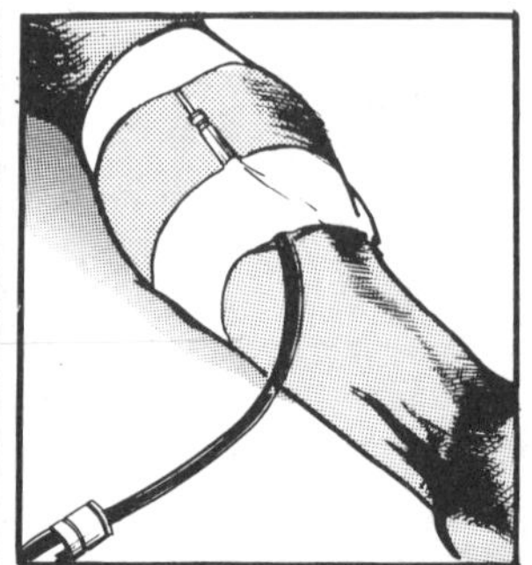
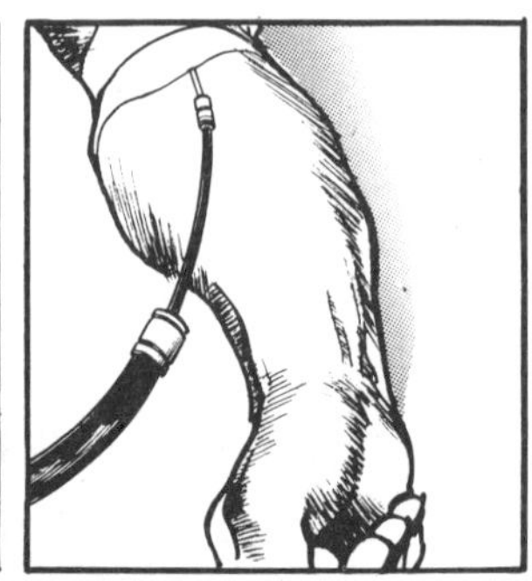
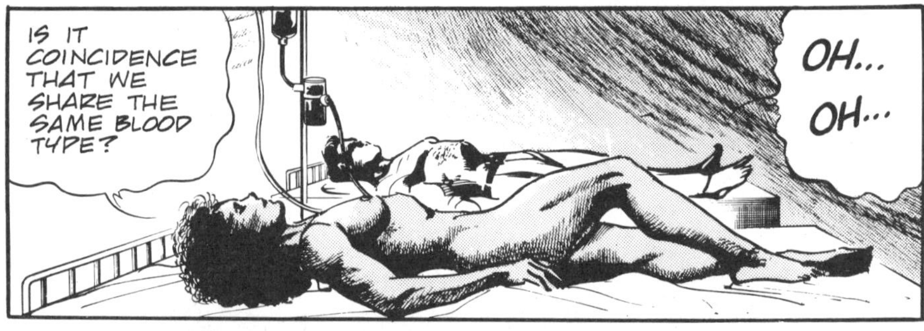
IS IT COINCIDENCE THAT WE SHARE THE SAME BLOOD TYPE?
OH... OH...

I FEEL LIKE I'M COMING...

Chapter 5

The Killing Ring Part 8

UH
UH
UH
UH
UH
UH

ARE YOU ALL RIGHT?
YES. I'M FINE.

IS THAT A SOUVENIR FOR YOUR WIFE?
YES.

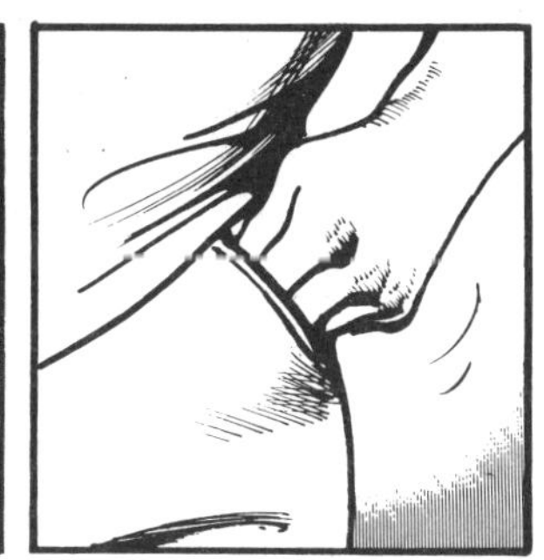

I WONDER WHAT KIND OF A WOMAN SHE IS.
SHE'S JAPANESE, ISN'T SHE ?
HER NAME IS FU CHING LAN.

Oooh

MAKE UP A NAME FOR ME. I'M TIRED OF BEING CALLED BUGNUG.

HM. I WILL CALL YOU DARK EYES.

DARK EYES... I LIKE IT.

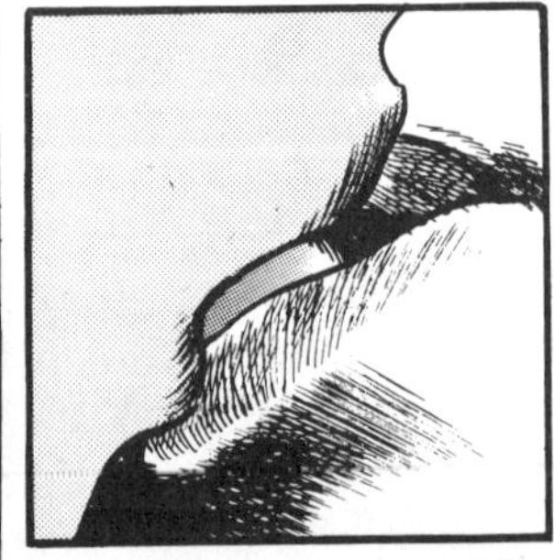
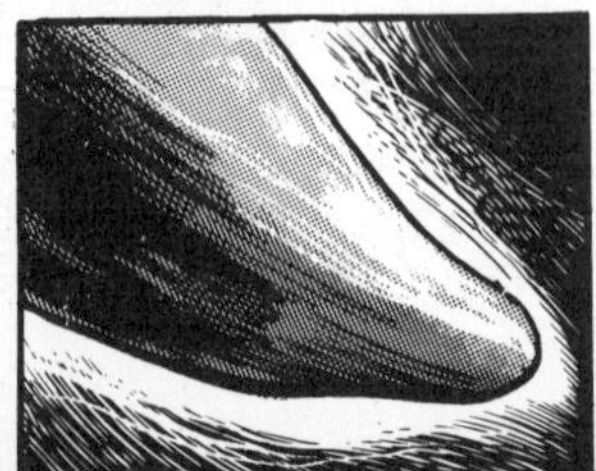

ARE YOU SURE YOU'RE ALL RIGHT? YOU MAY NOT BE WELL ENOUGH TO RUN...

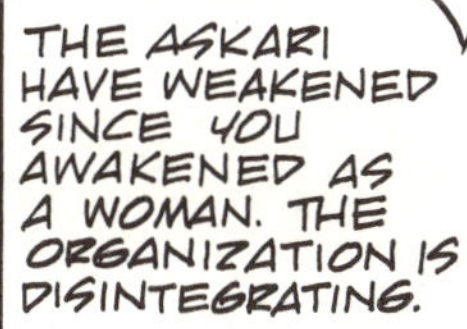
THE ASKARI HAVE WEAKENED SINCE YOU AWAKENED AS A WOMAN. THE ORGANIZATION IS DISINTEGRATING.
MANY OF YOUR MEN HAVE DESERTED, AND HALF OF THOSE WHO REMAIN HAVE TURNED AGAINST YOU.

IT WAS INEVITABLE.

BUT...
THERE'S NO DOUBT THAT THOSE WHO REMAIN INTEND TO KILL US AND SEIZE THE REIGNS OF POWER.

WHA-?

THIS AREA IS DANGEROUS.

SHUSH
SHUSH

COLT AUTHENTIC
9 M/M LUGER
AL
MAR

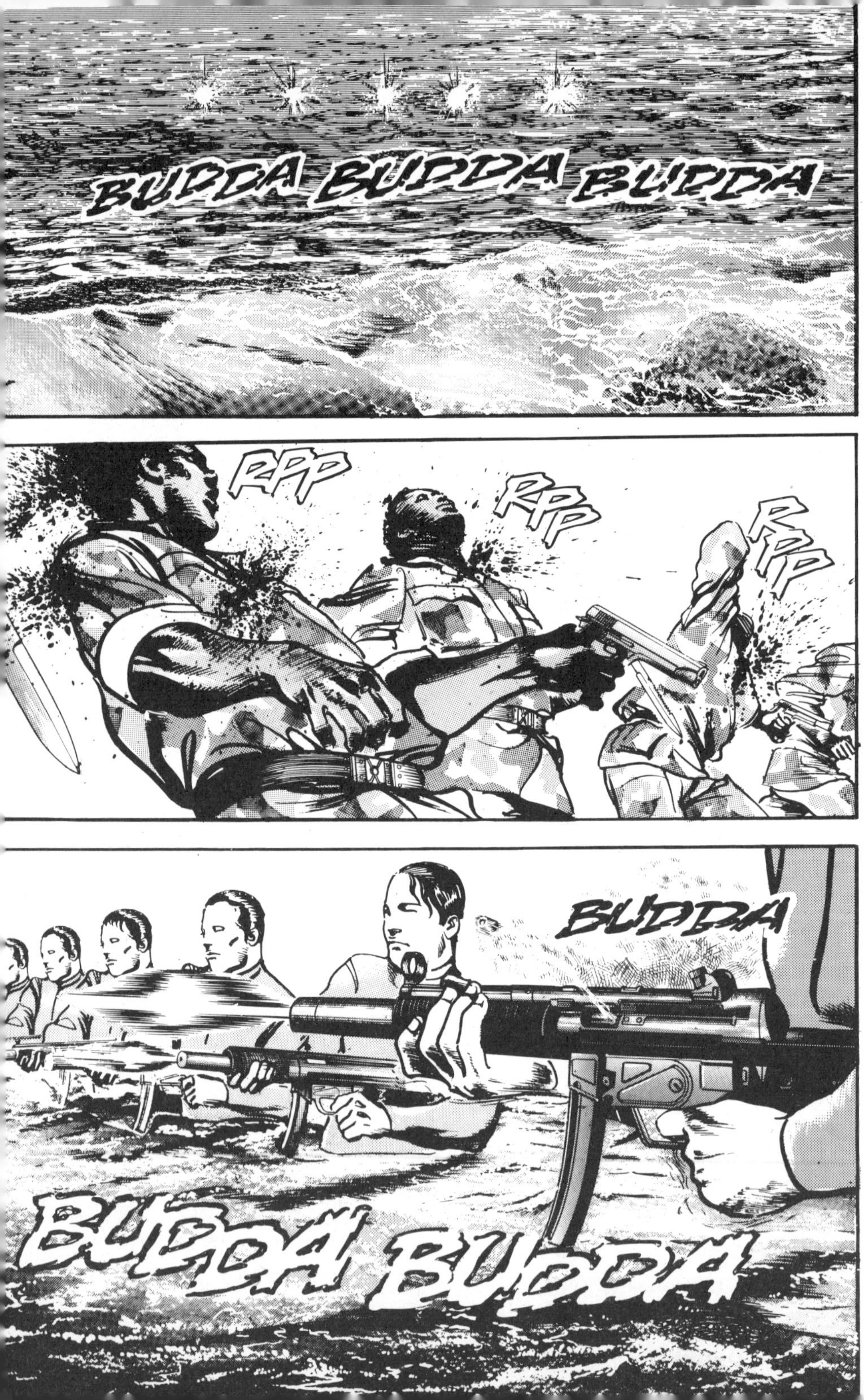

BUDDA

BUDDA BUDDA

BUDDA BUDDA
BUDDA

BUDDA
BUDDA
BUDDA

NOW I CAN LEAVE. THE REMAINING MEMBERS WILL OBEY YOU, DARK EYES.

OH...OH... PLEASE, DON'T FORGET ME.
OH...! YOUR BLOOD IS IN ME, AND MINE IS MIXED WITH YOURS!

OHHHHH!

WHEN... WHEN WILL I SEE YOU AGAIN ?

I WILL CALL YOU WHEN I NEED YOU.

MMMMMMMM

SHHHHHH

SHHHHHH

Haha
haha
ha
haha
haha

Haha
ha
hahaha

WHO WOULD HAVE THOUGHT THAT I, BUGNUG OF THE ASKARI, WOULD FALL IN LOVE WITH A MAN?
Hahahahaha!

WHP
WHP
WHP
WHP
WHP
WHP
WHP
WHP
WHP
WHP
I AM DARK EYES, THE WOMAN OF OM THAI YEUNG!

THMP
THMP

WHMPPP

SISTER!!

SISTER!

TAKE IT EASY, IVORY FAN. THINK OF YOUR WOUND.

I DON'T CARE ABOUT THAT. WE JUST HEARD FROM MY BROTHER. HE IS COMING HOME!

OHHH!

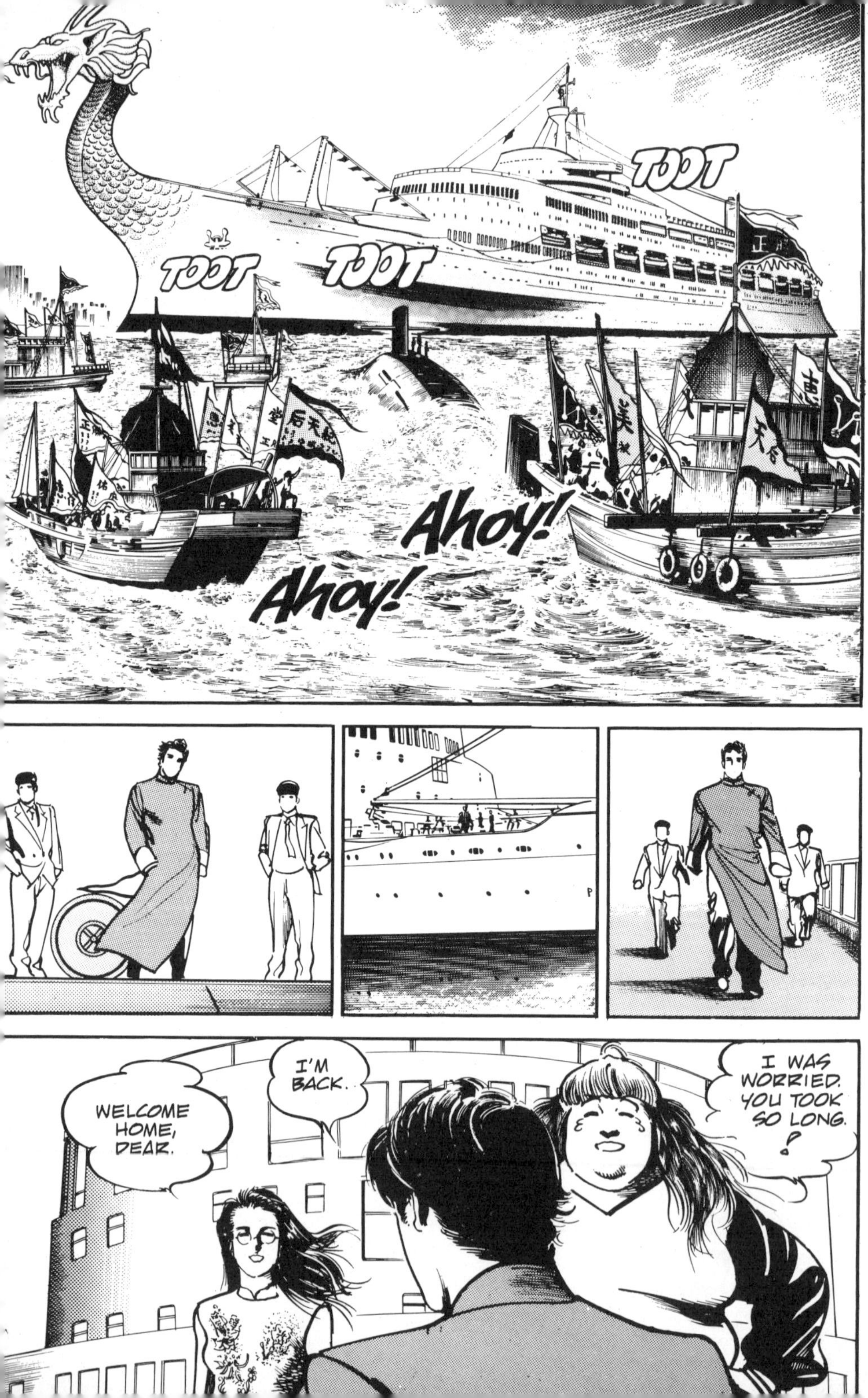

TOOT
TOOT
TOOT
Ahoy!
Ahoy!

HAVE YOU RECOVERED, IVORY FAN?
YES. I AM IMMORTAL.

I HAVE SETTLED EVERYTHING. THE OLD MEN CAN REST IN PEACE NOW.
I AM BACK, SIR.

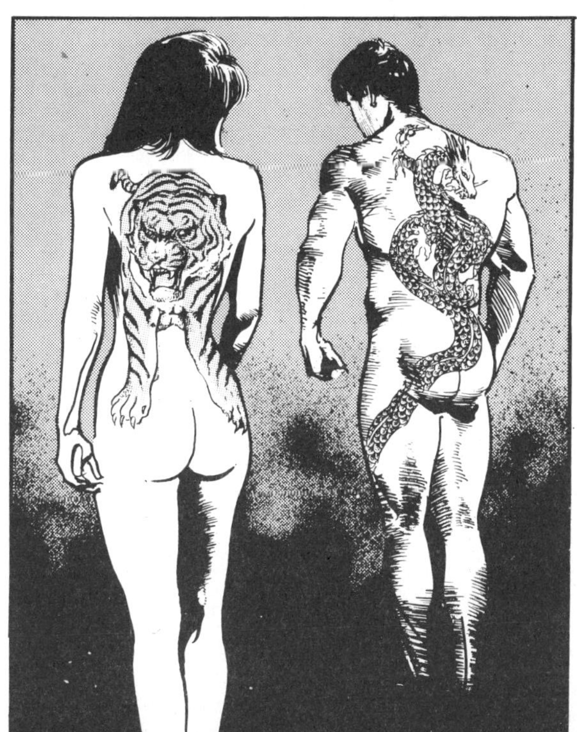

THE DRAGON AND THE TIGER ARE TOGETHER AGAIN AFTER A LONG TIME.

YES. I AM GLAD.

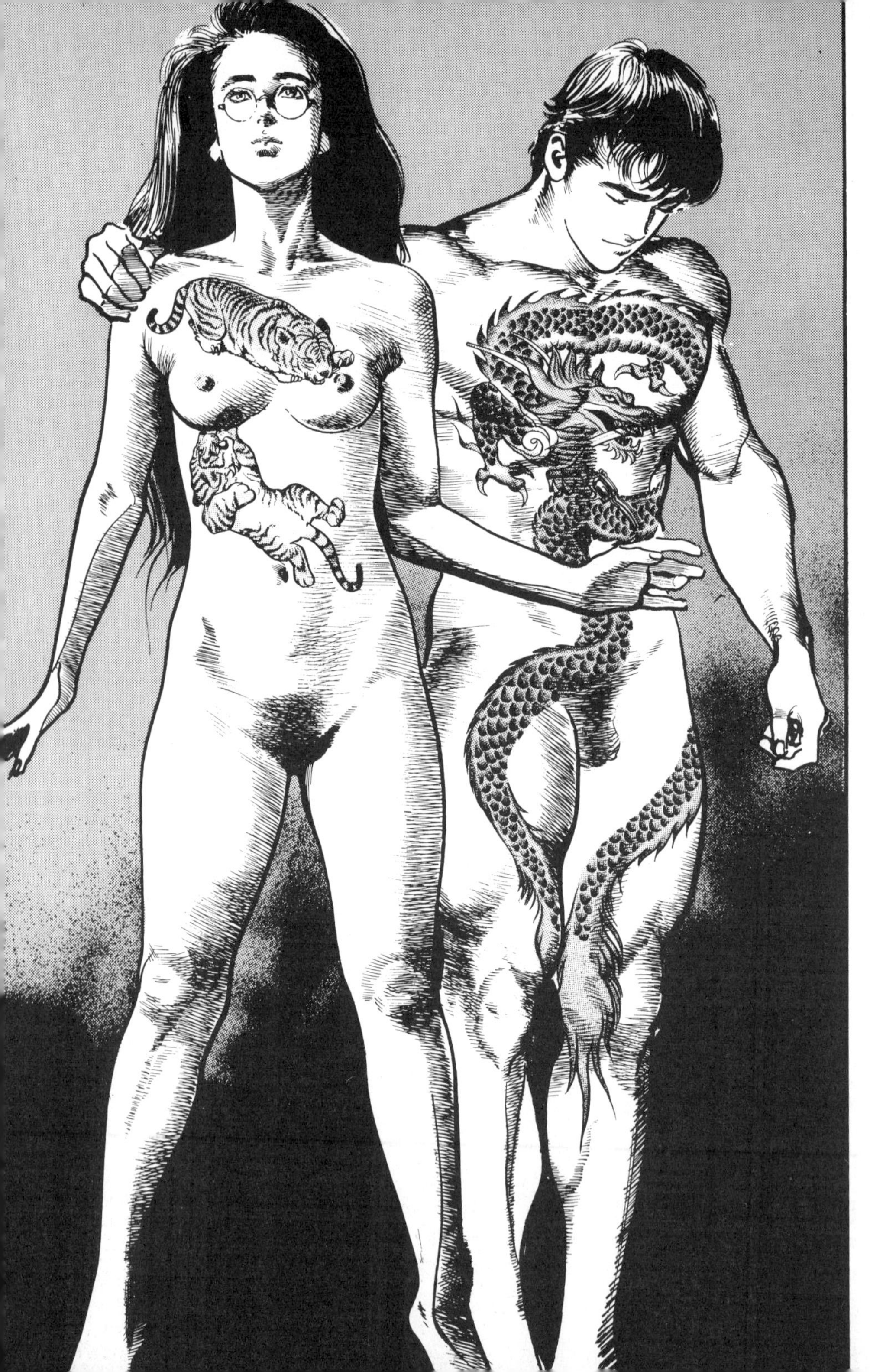

Chapter 6 Sister Part 1

OHHHHH
OH, DEAR... AGAIN...
HONEY...

BRRRRR
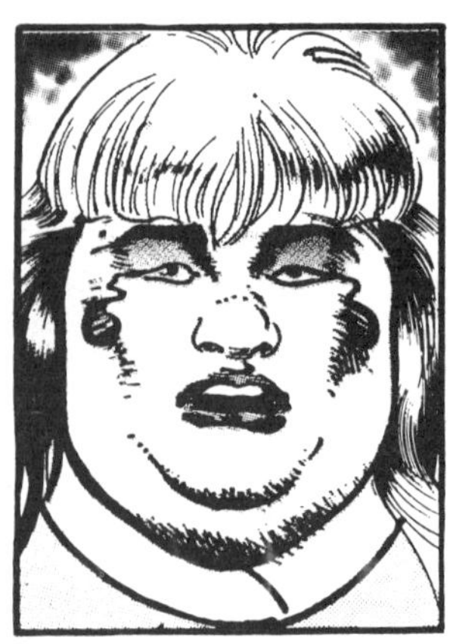

UH UH UH

COME, IVORY FAN. IT'S TIME TO ASK YOU TO WASH OFF OUR SWEAT.

YES, SISTER.

UH
UH
UH

WHAT AN UNUSUAL SIGHT!

IT'S AS IF THEY HAD MERGED SOULS.
CONJUGAL LOVE AND SISTERLY LOVE HAVE BECOME AS ONE.

THEY SHOW GREAT COMPASSION FOR IVORY FAN.
YES. TO WATCH THEM MAKE LOVE MAKES HER SUPREMELY HAPPY.

IVORY FAN HAD WORRIED US FOR QUITE SOME TIME, BUT I AM NO LONGER CONCERNED.
NOR I.

OHHHHHH
OH, I CAN'T HOLD BACK ANY LONGER! I'M... COMING...

BLUB
AHHHHHH
MMM
MMM

HE OFFERS THIS SOUVENIR AS A GIFT.
HIS NAME IS SHIRO KAIEDA.
HE HAS A GOOD LETTER OF INTRO-DUCTION. AND HE HAS UNDER-GONE A THOROUGH CHECK.

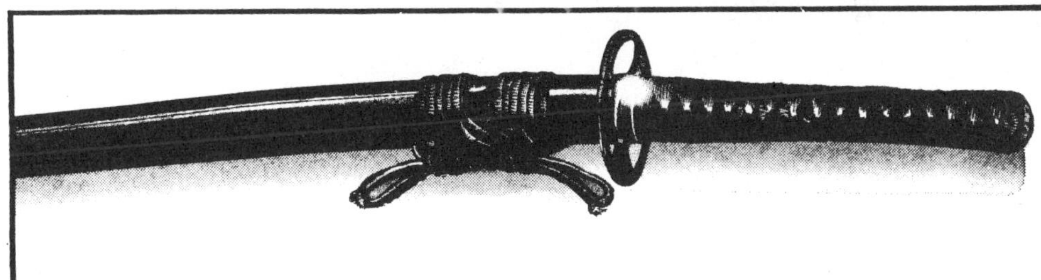

I AM HONORED TO MEET YOU, MR. OM.
THE SWORD'S NAME IS MURAMASA.

PLEASE, TAKE A LOOK AT IT.

KLINK
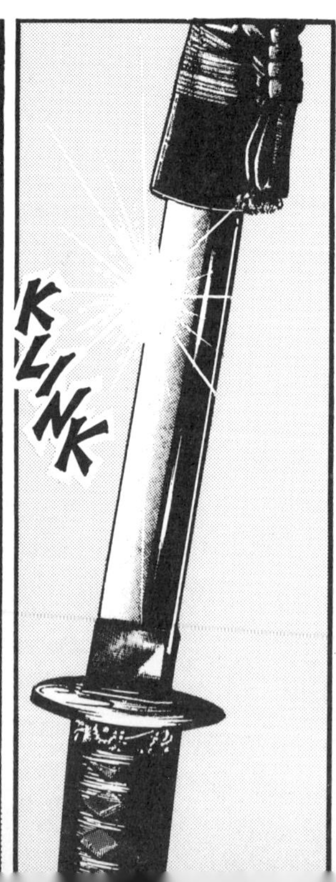
KLINK

IEYASU TOKUGAWA, THE FIRST SHOGUN, HELD THIS SWORD TO BE EVIL.

I HAVE HEARD TELL OF HOW MASAMUNE, ANOTHER LEGENDARY SWORD, WAS ONCE EMBEDDED IN A RIVER. A LEAF, BORNE BY THE CURRENT, WAS SEVERED IN HALF WHEN IT TOUCHED THE BLADE, AND BOTH HALVES WERE CARRIED DOWN STREAM.
IN MURAMASA'S CASE, IT ALSO CUT A LEAF IN HALF, BUT BOTH HALVES REMAINED STUCK TO THE BLADE.

MURAMASA IS A VERY PRECIOUS SWORD. IN JAPAN, IT IS VALUED AT TWO HUNDRED MILLION YEN.
WE OFFER IT AS A TOKEN FOR YOUR HELP.

THE 108 DRAGONS...
...ACCEPT PAYMENTS IN CASH ONLY. PLEASE, LEAVE.

PLEASE GIVE ME A CHANCE TO DEMONSTRATE MURAMASA'S SHARPNESS.

NOT NECESSARY.

IS THAT SO?

Ha Ha Ha Ha Ha

I DID NOT EXPECT THINGS TO GO AS SMOOTHLY AS I WISHED.

HE WHO HAS MASTERED THE ICHIDEN SCHOOL OF DRAWING A SWORD COVERS AN AREA SIX METERS WIDE.
HA HA HA HA. IN OTHER WORDS, EVERYTHING WITHIN A RADIUS OF THREE METERS WILL BE CUT IN HALF BY ONE STROKE OF MY SWORD.

SHIIIIST

KLINK

PNNNK

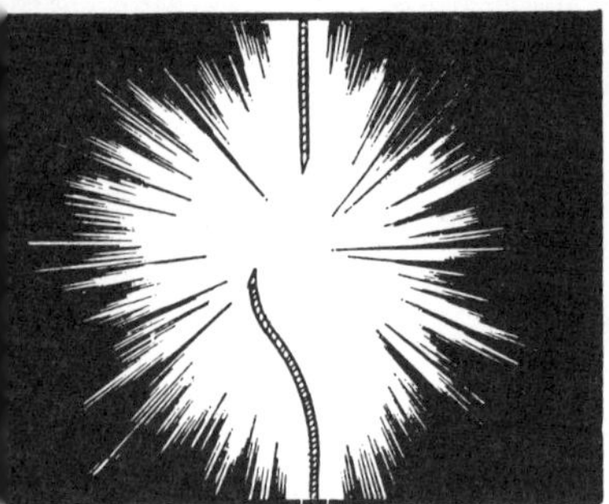

HAHA
IT SEEMS THAT TIME HAS RUN OUT FOR FREEMAN, THE FOREMOST ASSASSIN OF THE CENTURY.

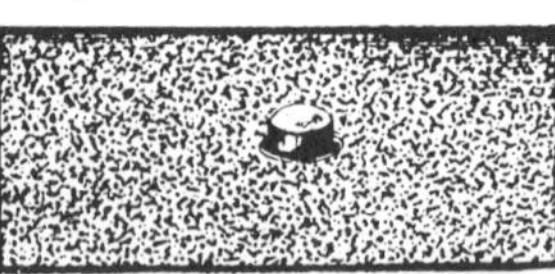

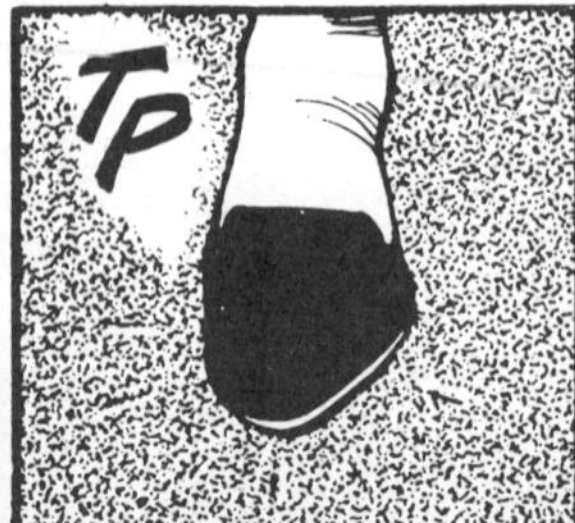
TP

WHUUUMP

SUSH
SUSH
SUSH
SUSH

WHOOOOSH
WHIIIISH
SPLSHH
Thnk

SHSH

SWISH SWISH
UGHHHH

ARE YOU TERMINALLY ILL?

I ONLY HAVE SIX MONTHS TO LIVE... BUT, HOW?

YOU HAVE SHOWED OFF YOUR SKILL...
THE OSTENTATIOUS SELF-INDULGENCE OF A DYING MAN. IT WAS EVIDENT THAT YOU DID NOT EXPECT TO LEAVE HERE ALIVE.

...GOOD GUESS...

I WILL RETURN THE SWORD FOR YOU. WHERE IS YOUR FAMILY?

I DO NOT HAVE... A FAMILY.

UGHH

Chapter 6 Sister Part 2

EEEEEEEEEE

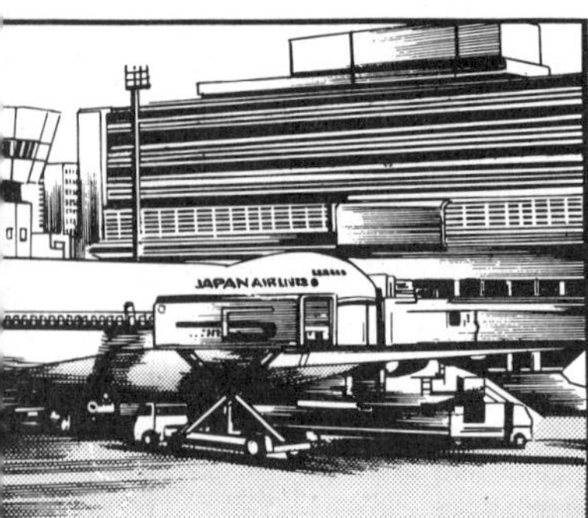
JAPAN AIR LINES

PROFESSOR !!

YES! YES!

I'VE NOT SEEN YOU FOR SO LONG, PROFESSOR. FORGIVE ME FOR NOT WRITING.
SAME HERE. YOU'VE BECOME EVEN MORE BEAUTIFUL!

I HEARD THAT YOU MARRIED A NATIVE OF THIS LAND. YOU LOOK VERY HAPPY.

I AM IVORY FAN, HER LITTLE SISTER.
HA HA!
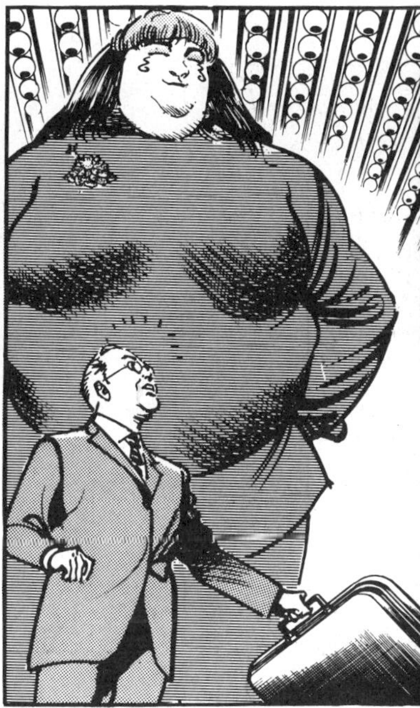

YES, SHE IS.
SHE'S MY BIG LITTLE SISTER.

I AM PLEASED TO MEET MY SISTER'S PROFESSOR FROM HER DAYS AT THE UNIVERSITY.

RRRRRRM

Whp Whp

YOUR MANNER OF SERVING TEA IS EXCELLENT.

THANK YOU VERY MUCH, PROFESSOR MIKAGE. WOULD YOU LIKE ANOTHER CUP?

YES, PLEASE.

I ALSO WOULD LIKE ANOTHER CUP, PLEASE.

KISSSH

YOU ARE LUCKY, EMU. YOU HAVE A WONDERFUL HUSBAND.

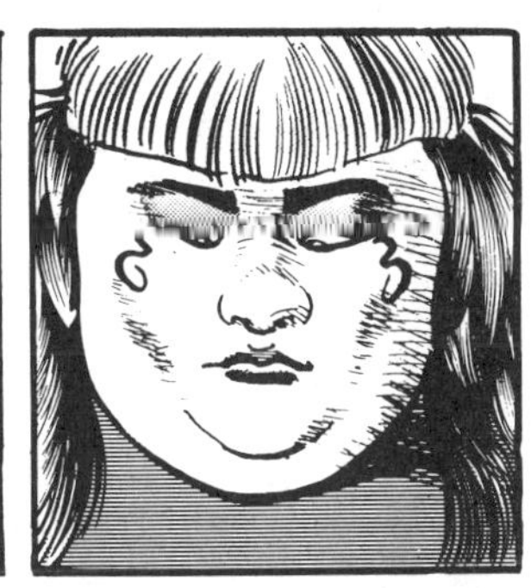

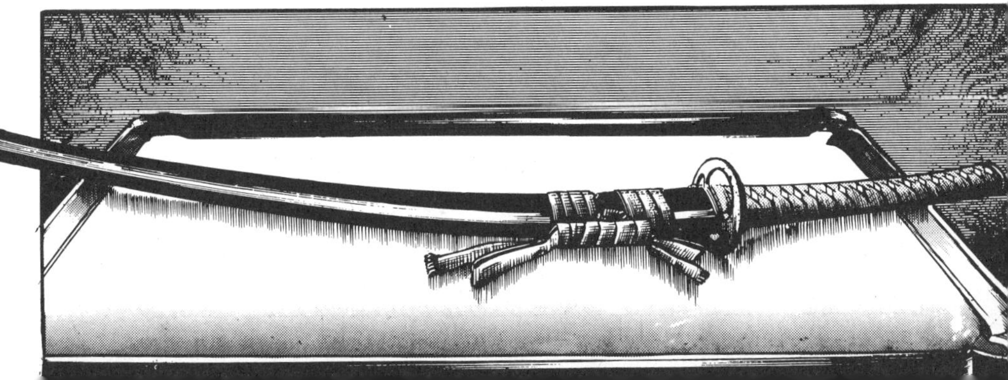

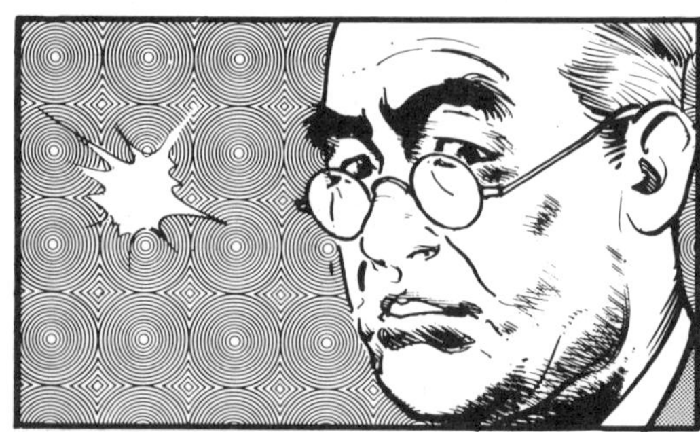

IT... IT CAN'T BE... IT CAN'T BE MURAMASA, THE DEVIL'S SWORD!

LET'S SEE...

KLINK

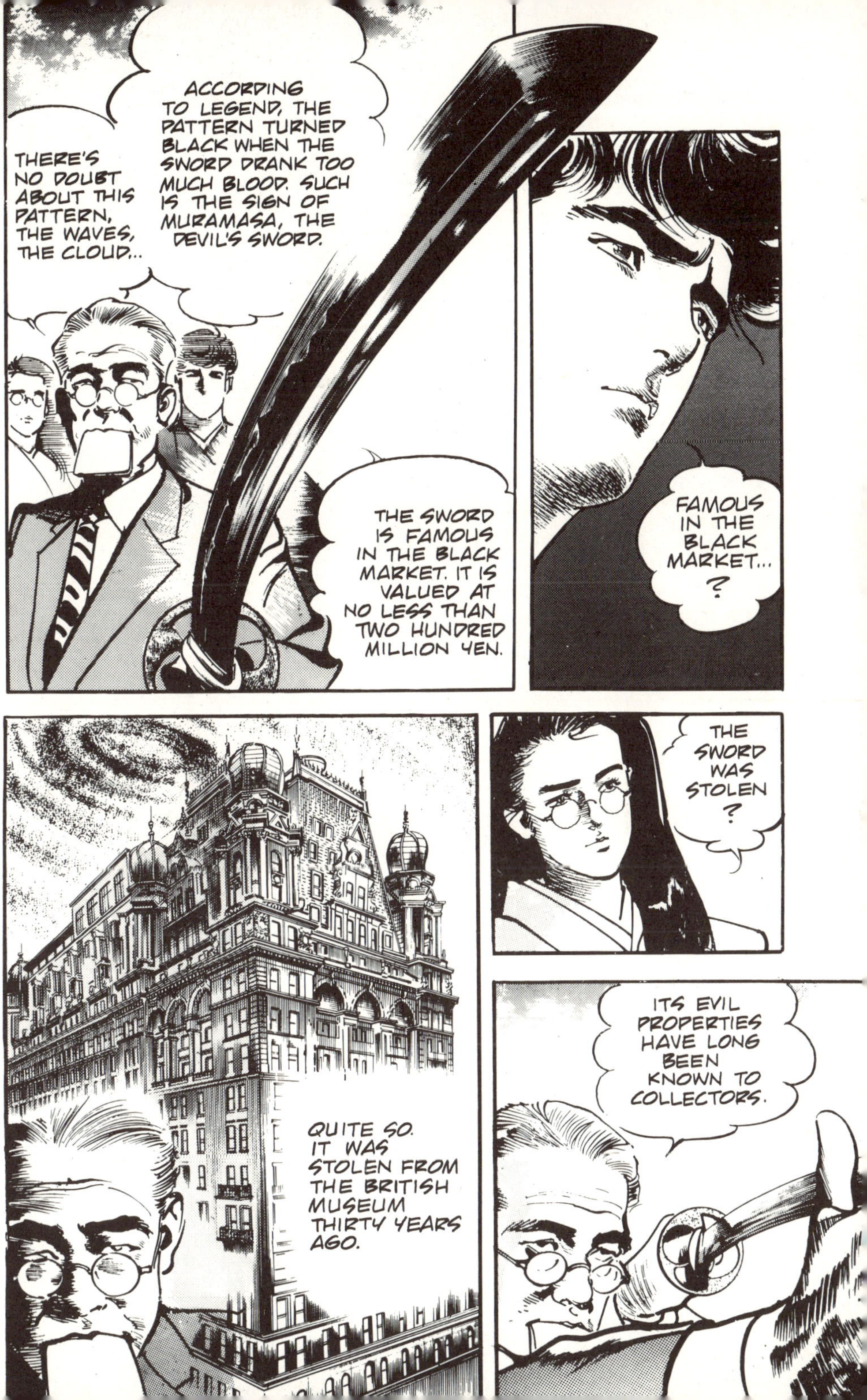

THERE'S NO DOUBT ABOUT THIS PATTERN, THE WAVES, THE CLOUD...

ACCORDING TO LEGEND, THE PATTERN TURNED BLACK WHEN THE SWORD DRANK TOO MUCH BLOOD. SUCH IS THE SIGN OF MURAMASA, THE DEVIL'S SWORD.

THE SWORD IS FAMOUS IN THE BLACK MARKET. IT IS VALUED AT NO LESS THAN TWO HUNDRED MILLION YEN.

FAMOUS IN THE BLACK MARKET... ?

THOSE WHO SEARCH FOR SUCH ITEMS HAUNT WHAT'S KNOWN AS THE BLACK MARKET OF ARTS.
IT IS SAID THAT WHOEVER OUTBIDS OTHERS FOR THE SWORD WILL DIE.
IT CERTAINLY DOOMED THE TOKUGAWA SHOGUNATE. ACCORDING TO HISTORY, NO ONE WHO OWNED IT SURVIVED.
IT DOOMED EVERYONE.
TING
鬼包丁村正
THE DEVIL'S SWORD, MURAMASA.

THIS HAS BEEN AN UNPLEASANT ENCOUNTER. THE SWORD CAN NEITHER BE OWNED NOR DISCARDED. HE WHO LETS IT GO IS DOUBLY CURSED.

CHKK

WHOOSH

KLINK

ALLEGEDLY, A MAN ONCE TRIED TO BREAK THE SWORD.
HE FEARED THAT SOMEONE WOULD FIND THE SWORD IF HE MERELY THREW IT AWAY, AND WOULD HENCE COME TO HARM.

BUT MURAMASA DID NOT BREAK. IT RECOILED AND EMBEDDED ITSELF IN THE MAN'S CHEST.

SHHHHHH
SPLASH

Ahhhh

SPLSSH
SPLSSH
SPLSSH

SPLOOOOSH

THNNK
THRSSH
THRSSH
CLNKK
Oh Oh Oh Oh
BRRRR
I HAVE NO CHOICE BUT TO BELIEVE THE STORIES WHICH THE BLACK MARKET OF ARTS HAS HANDED DOWN.

AHHHH

WHAT HAPPENED ?

WE FOUND THIS SHEATH IN THE BILGE WHEN WE PUMPED OUT WATER WHILE CLEANING THE ENGINE ROOM.
I THOUGHT IT WAS SO BEAUTIFUL...

YOU WILL BRING HARM TO YOURSELF IF YOU TRY TO ABANDON IT AGAIN.
YOU JUST CAN'T GET RID OF IT!

ARE YOU THE PRESENT OWNER ?

I AM.

AHH

SISTER!

MMM
PLEASE, DON'T WORRY. EITHER OF YOU.

KLINK

Chapter 6 Sister Part 3

KISSSH
RRRRM

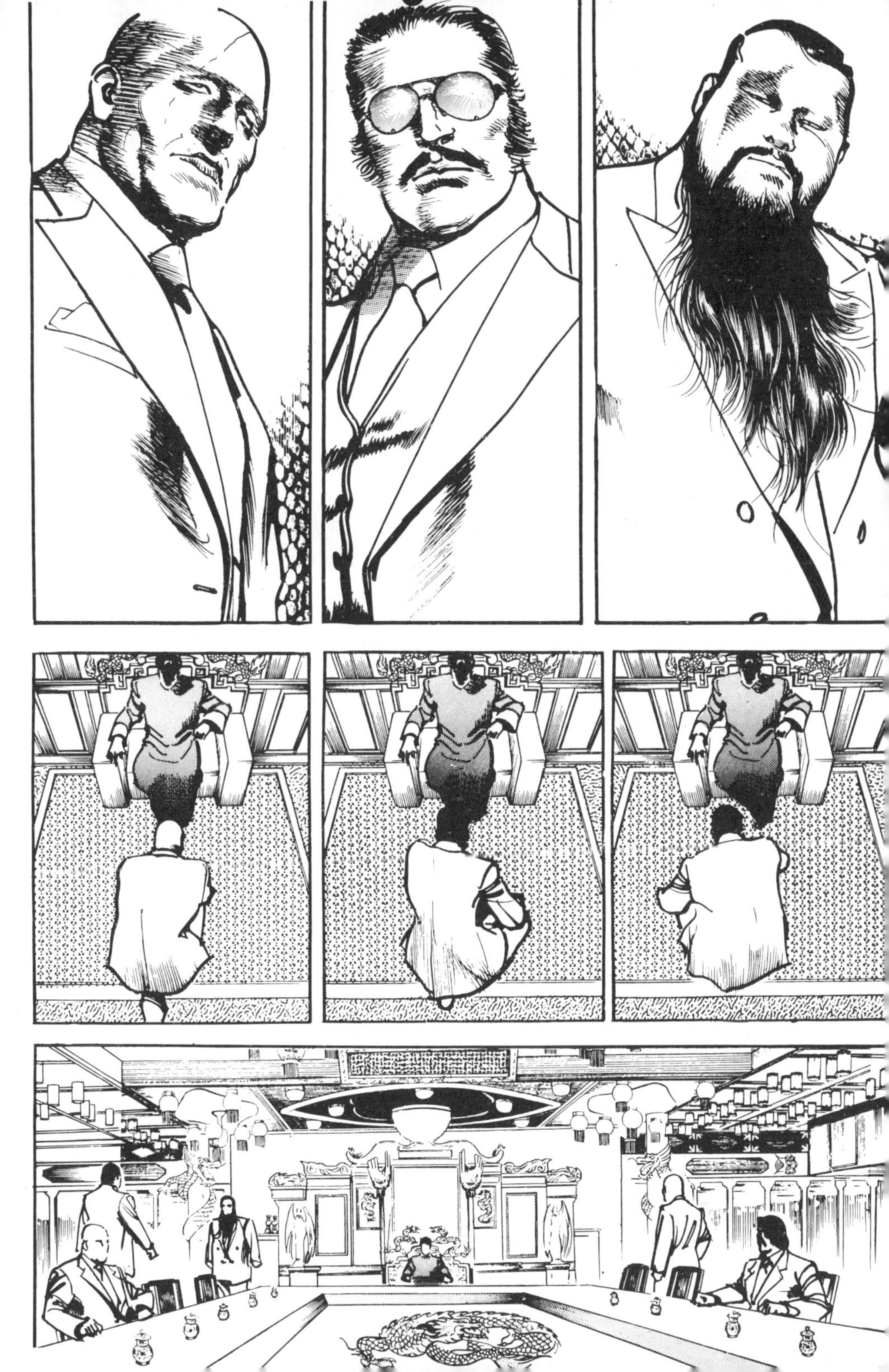

WHP
WHP
WHP
WHP
WHP
SSSSS

WHRRR

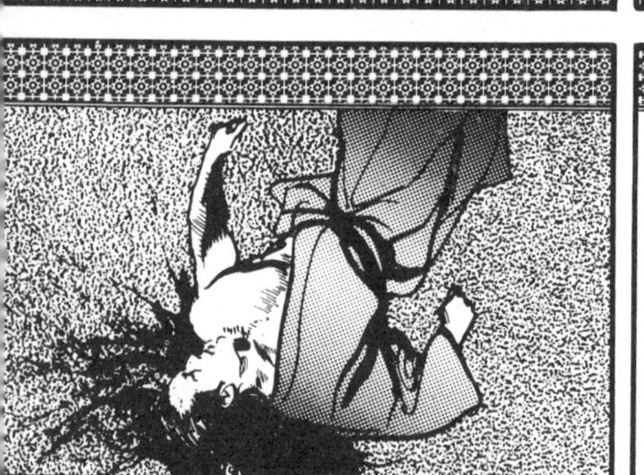

KLK

KLK

SHIRO KAIEDA'S LETTER OF INTRODUCTION WAS WRITTEN ON SPECIAL PAPER WHICH BORE THE WATERMARK OF THE 108 DRAGONS.
THE LETTER WAS WRITTEN BY MR. IMAIDA, THE CHAIRMAN OF KANTO RAILWAY, WHO SUPPORTS OUR ORGANI-ZATION.
THAT IS HOW I CAME TO MEET KAIEDA.

BUT WE HAVE JUST LEARNED THAT MR. IMAIDA IS MISSING.
FOUR DAYS AGO HE WAS KIDNAPPED FROM HIS SUMMER HOUSE ON THE IZU PENINSULA.

SOMEONE IS ACTIVELY TRYING TO DESTROY THE ORGA-NIZATION OF THE 108 DRAGONS.

HMMM

AND THE EPICENTER OF THIS UNKNOWN MOVEMENT...
...IS PROBABLY...

...IN JAPAN !

MMMM

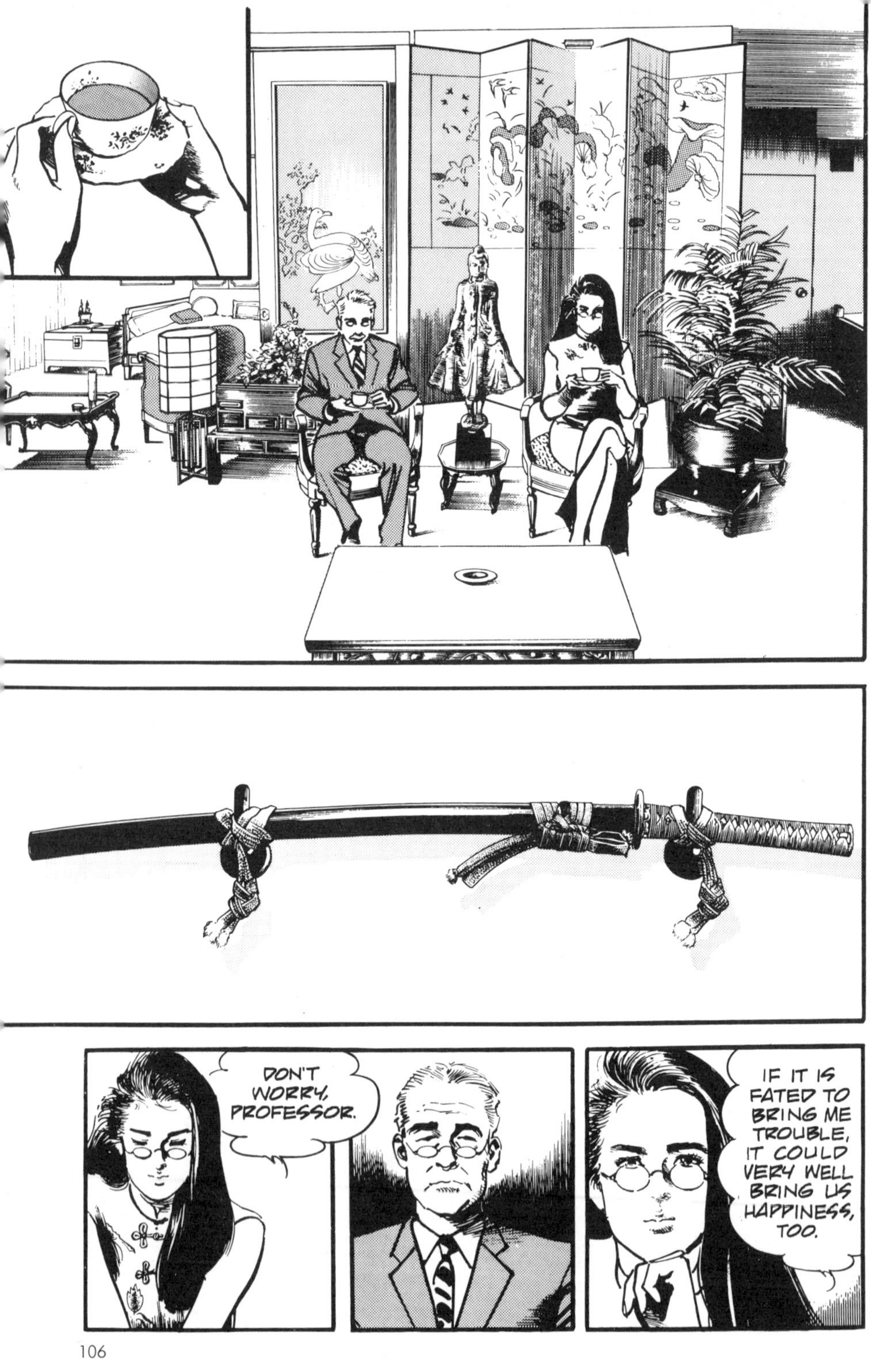

DON'T WORRY, PROFESSOR.

IF IT IS FATED TO BRING ME TROUBLE, IT COULD VERY WELL BRING US HAPPINESS, TOO.

I THINK PEOPLE FIND THE SWORD REPELLENT BECAUSE THEY FEAR AND ALIENATE IT.

IF SOMEONE WOULD UNDERSTAND THE CURSE CONFINED IN THE SWORD...
...AND TRY TO LOVE AND COMFORT IT, AS IF IT POSSESSED A SOUL...
...THAT SOMEONE WOULD PROBABLY COME TO NO HARM.

DO YOU BELIEVE THAT?

TO LOVE AND HONOR THE SWORD DOES NOT MEAN...
...THAT ONE SHOULD SLEEP WITH IT OR CLEAN IT.

WHAT IT MEANS IS TO DRAW IT JUST SO, AND WIELD IT JUST SO, AND TO ATTACK LIKE THE VERY WIND.
LEFT TO LESSER HANDS, MURAMASA CAN ONLY BE REPELLENT.
ONLY A MASTER SWORDSMAN CAN SUCCEED.
IT HAS NEVER BEEN TREATED PROPERLY AS A SWORD, BUT VALUED AS A MERE TREASURE. ONE WHO DOES NOT UNDERSTAND IT LIVES IN BONDAGE TO IT.

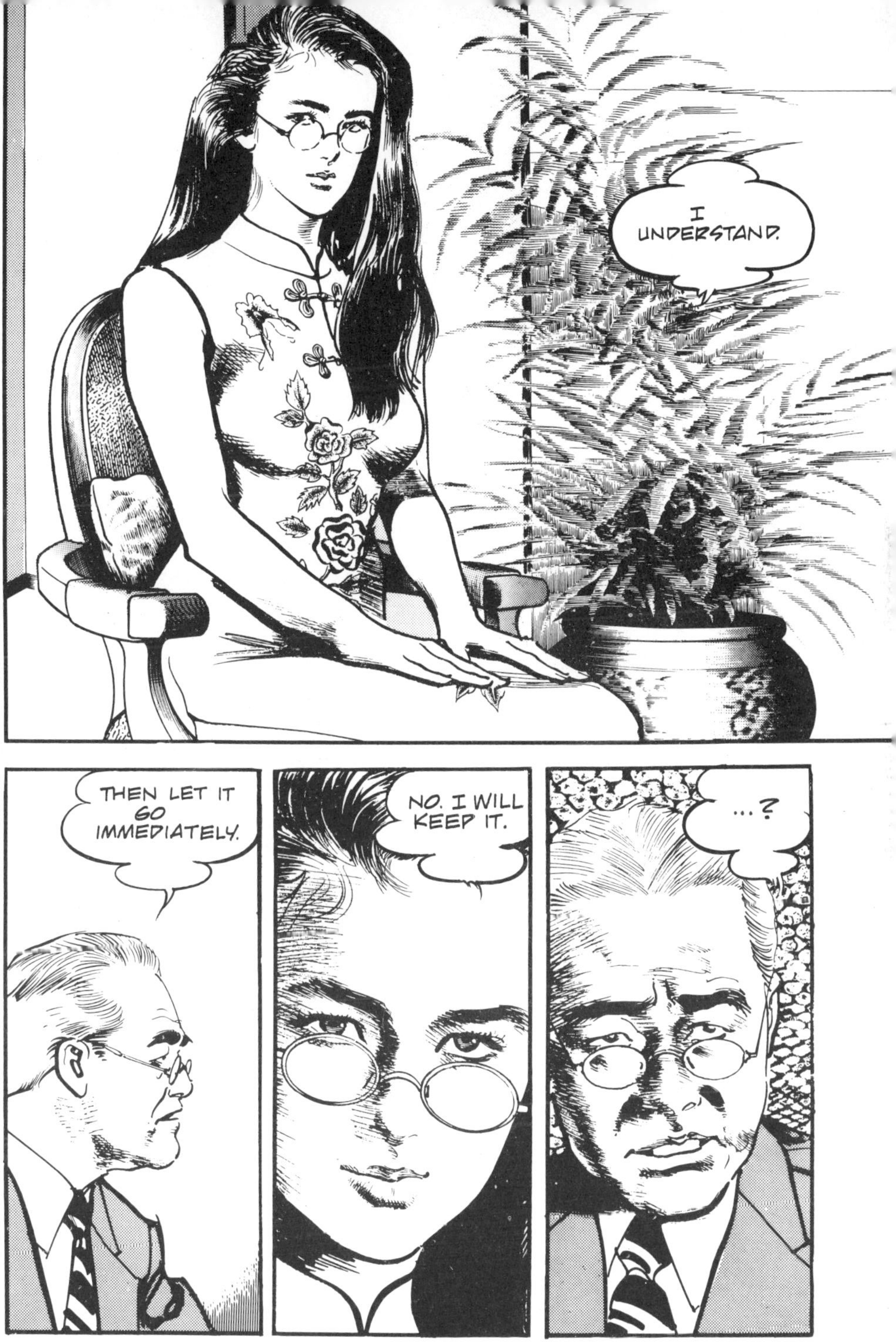

I UNDERSTAND.

I SUSPECTED SOMEONE WAS BEHIND THE ASKARI.

BUGNUG DOESN'T KNOW WHO HE WAS.

SHE ONLY HEARD THAT SHIKEBARO AND JIGON WERE IN CONTACT WITH SOMEONE IN JAPAN.

WHY DID THE ASKARI CHALLENGE US?

THE MOTIVE WAS NEVER CLEAR.

I HAVE A FEELING THAT WHOEVER WAS BEHIND THE ASKARI IS CONNECTED WITH THIS MURAMASA INCIDENT.

ORDERS, EVERYONE!

USE ALL OUR RESOURCES, FIND OUT THE IDENTITY OF WHOEVER HAS RISEN AGAINST OUR ORGANIZATION.

BUGNUG, YOU COMMAND THE OPERATION!

DARK EYES.

YES, SIR.

LEAVE FOR JAPAN!

YES, FREEMAN.

Hmmm

THEY PROBABLY DON'T KNOW THAT YOU'RE ON OUR SIDE NOW.

RRRRRRRM

SISTER
!

YES
?

WE WILL ARRIVE AT KOWLOON CASTLE SOON. I CAN'T BELIEVE IT...

BUT... BUT WHY ?
DO. WE ARE GOING TO KOWLOON CASTLE.

BECAUSE I UNDERSTAND THAT A MASTER SWORDSMAN DWELLS IN KOWLOON CASTLE.

I WILL LEARN SWORDS-MANSHIP, AND MASTER THE ART.
AND I WILL LOVE AND CHERISH MURAMASA. I WILL CLEAVE THE AIR, AND SUMMON THE WIND.

THEN MURAMASA WILL NOT BRING ME BAD LUCK. NOR TEARS, NOR TURMOIL.
I HAVE COME TO THAT UNDERSTANDING.

WHO IS THIS MASTER SWORDSMAN?
WHAT IS HE CALLED?

I DO NOT KNOW MUCH ABOUT HIM. HIS NAME IS GOKEN ISHIDA. PROFESSOR MIKAGE SAID HE MUST BE CLOSE TO SEVENTY YEARS OF AGE.
BUT WE CAN BE CERTAIN THAT HE IS IN KOWLOON CASTLE.

RRRR RRM

NO! WE MUSTN'T GO THERE! EVEN THE 108 DRAGONS HAVE NO POWER OVER KOWLOON CASTLE!
THE PLACE IS DESERTED.
IT IS HELL ON EARTH!

LET'S GO HOME, SISTER. WE MUSTN'T GO TO THE HOME OF THE LIVING DEAD!
RRRRRRM
I MYSELF WILL FIND YOU ANOTHER TEACHER!

YOU MUST COME!!

HMMPH

WE HAVE TO GO THERE, IVORY FAN!

Y-Y-YES...

RRRRM

MMMMMMMM
JAPAN AIR LINES

Chapter 6 Sister Part 4

RRRRRRM

GOVERNMENT LAND
NO ENTRY AND NO DUMPING
政府土地
不准進入
不准倒垃圾

pt pt pt

THIS PLACE IS NO GOOD!
WHEN I WAS GROWING UP, I WAS TOLD THAT I WOULD BE DUMPED ON KOWLOON CASTLE IF I DIDN'T BEHAVE.

FORTY THOUSAND PEOPLE LIVE HERE. NEITHER ENGLAND, CHINA, NOR HONG KONG CLAIMS IT AS THEIR OWN.
IT'S AN EXTRATERRITORIAL SLUM AT THE ROOT OF THE KOWLOON PENINSULA.
NO ONE WILL ACKNOWLEGE THAT ANYBODY LIVES THERE.
MMMM

HMm
YES. NOW, LET US GO FIND MASTER GOKEN ISHIDA.

MURAMASA WILL HELP US.

BUT HOW ?

.....?

HE MUST KNOW OF MURAMASA IF HE IS JAPANESE AND A MASTER SWORDSMAN.
HE CANNOT IGNORE THIS SWORD. THE SPARK IN HIS EYES WILL BETRAY HIM.

PERHAPS...

WHAT SHALL WE DO WITH THE BOAT, SISTER? I HAVE A FEELING IT WILL BE DESTROYED IF WE LEAVE IT HERE.

OH, YES.

KA-PLASH

KRAKK
KRAKK

THE BOTTOM IS VERY MUDDY. ANYBODY WHO TRIES TO GET AT THE BOAT WILL GET STUCK.

WHAT ABOUT US?

OH, YEAH.
Ha Ha Ha Ha Ha
Ha Ha Ha Ha

KISSHH

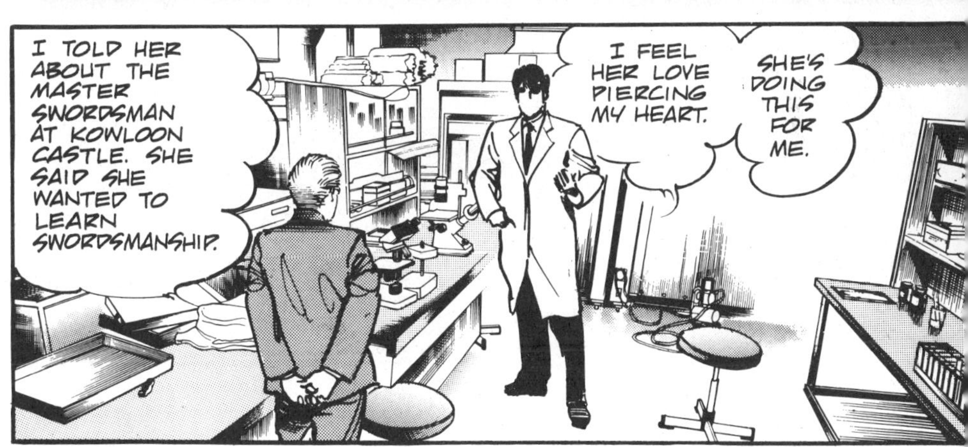
I TOLD HER ABOUT THE MASTER SWORDSMAN AT KOWLOON CASTLE. SHE SAID SHE WANTED TO LEARN SWORDSMANSHIP.
I FEEL HER LOVE PIERCING MY HEART.
SHE'S DOING THIS FOR ME.

SHE INSISTS ON OWNING MURAMASA SO THAT THE BURDEN WILL NOT FALL ON ME.
IF ANY HARM IS DONE, SHE DOES NOT WISH ME TO BEAR IT. THAT IS HOW SHE EXPRESSES HER LOVE.
HMMMM
LET HER DO AS SHE WISHES.
THAT IS HOW I EXPRESS MINE.

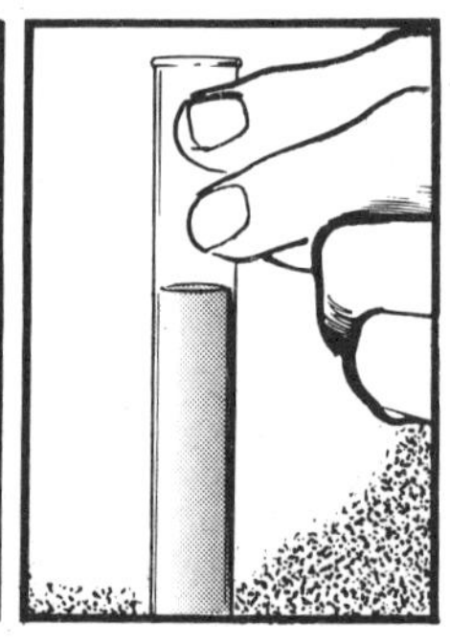

OUR LAB HAS RECENTLY DEVELOPED THIS FORMULA TO PROTECT THE STOMACH WALL.

GLLB

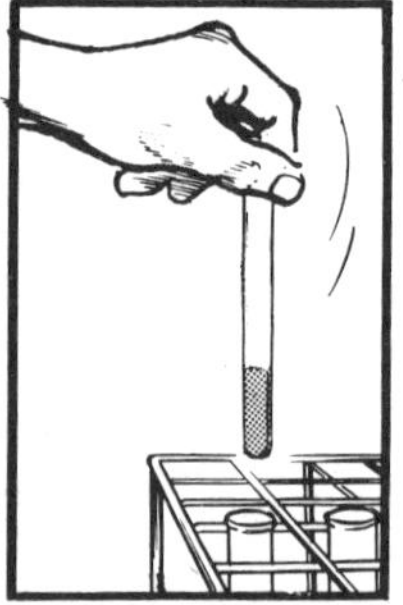

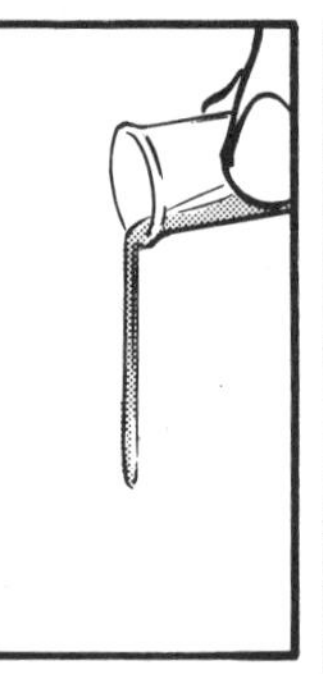

THIS IS HYDROCYANIC ACID.

GLB

NOOOOO

GLP

I'M OKAY. THE FORMULA COATED MY THROAT, GULLET, AND STOMACH WALL WITH A STRONG FILM.
IT SHUTS OUT ALL THE POISON.

IT LASTS FOR TWENTY MINUTES.

IN THE MEANTIME...

ARGGGGGG
GHHHHHH
PHEEEW

AFTER VOMITING AND GARGLING, YOU DRINK THIS ANTIDOTE.
THEN, THE POISON WILL NOT KILL YOU.

HMMMM

I'M SORRY THAT I SCARED YOU.
SINCE WE DON'T KNOW HOW OUR ENEMY WILL ATTACK, WE MUST PREPARE FOR ANY CONTINGENCY.

IT IS A WORLD BEYOND MY IMAGINATION.

YES. I WILL EXPLAIN ALL, PROFESSOR.
SO THAT YOU WILL TRULY UNDERSTAND US.

THERE'S SUPPOSED TO BE A HOTEL HERE CALLED BLUE KOWLOON GATE. I WAS TOLD THAT I COULD GET SOME INFORMATION AT THE FRONT DESK.
AGGGGH
KLIISH
AIEEEE

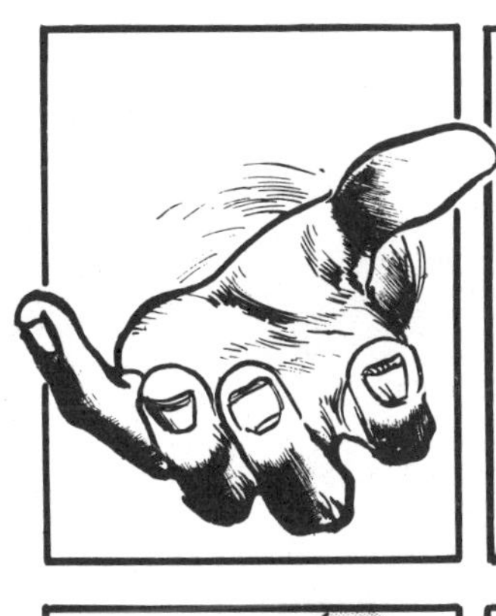

IS THERE A DOCTOR AROUND HERE?
KONG KONG

TP TP TP

SISTER !!

蕭秉陞牙科
志青診所

NO! THIS IS A DENTIST'S OFFICE!

TREAT THIS CHILD!

SURE. LAY HIM ON THE TABLE.

三鞭
海狗丸
IT DIDN'T REACH HIS HEART. HE'LL BE OKAY.
SLMMM

SHE'S PRETTY. WE CAN GET A GOOD PRICE FOR HER.

Chapter 6 Sister Part 5

GRRRR

COME HERE, YOU TWO. WE'LL HAVE US A LITTLE FUN BEFORE WE SELL YOU ON THE SLAVE MARKET.

DON'T MOVE! DO YOU WANT TO DIE?

YAAA
SLIIIVSH
ARGGGH
BUDDA
BUDDA

SLISH
ARGGGH

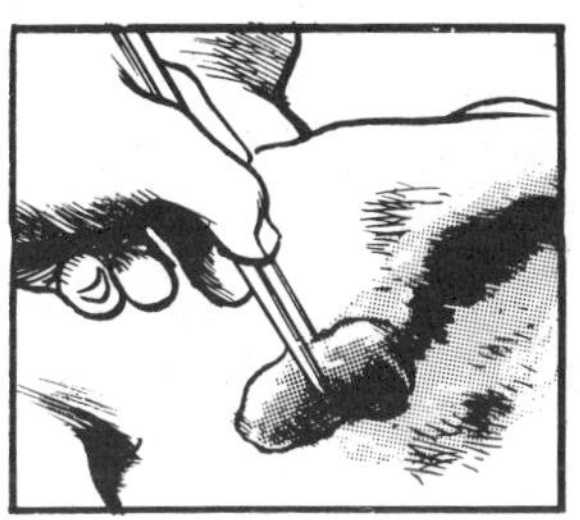
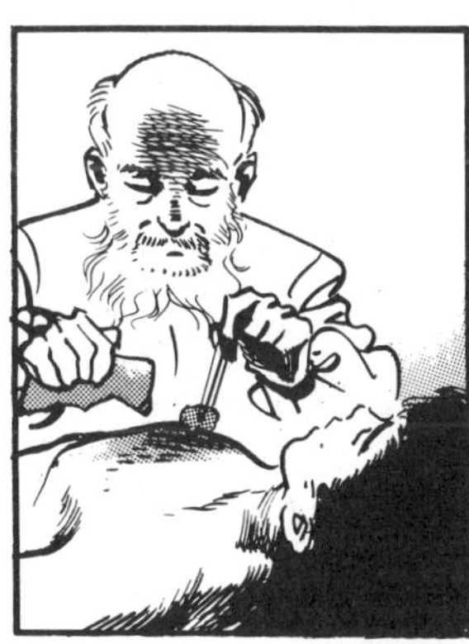

GOOD!! I STOPPED THE BLEEDING. HE'LL BE ALL RIGHT.

IF AT ALL POSSIBLE, I ONLY WANTED TO WOUND THEM.
BUT THEY GAVE ME NO CHOICE.
STILL, I DID MANAGE TO SPARE THREE LIVES, EVEN THOUGH THREE HAD TO DIE. I SUPPOSE IT EVENS OUT.

YOU MUST BE MASTER GOKEN ISHIDA.

HMMMM

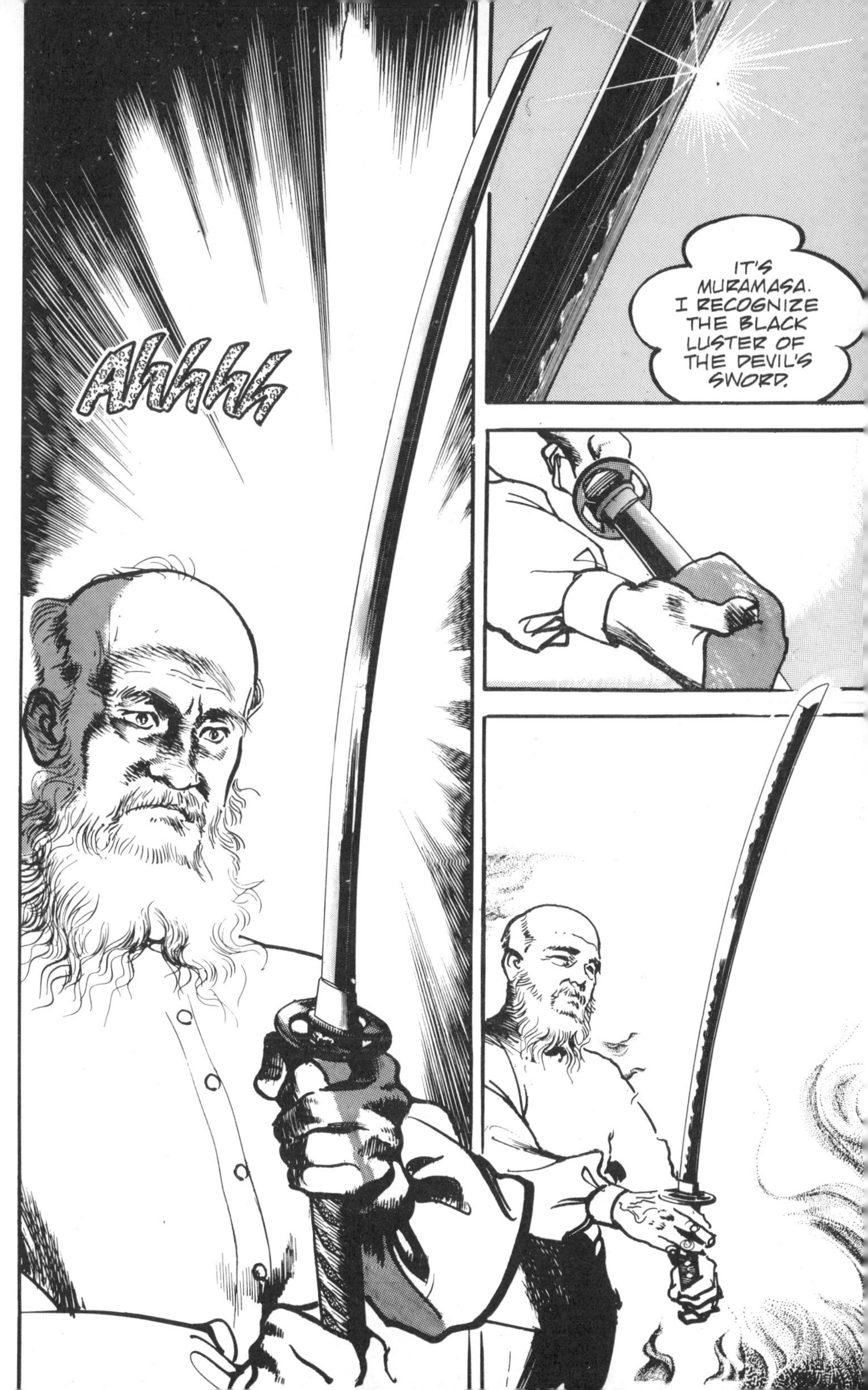
IT'S MURAMASA. I RECOGNIZE THE BLACK LUSTER OF THE DEVIL'S SWORD.
Ahhhh

MY NAME IS FU CHING LAN. I AM THE WIFE OF OM THAI YEUNG, WHO LEADS THE 108 DRAGONS.
I AM JAPANESE. MY NAME WAS EMU HINO BEFORE I MARRIED.

I WOULD LIKE YOU TO TEACH ME SWORDSMANSHIP...
...SO THAT I MAY BE MURAMASA'S TRUE MASTER.

WHY?

BECAUSE I WISH TO SPARE MY HUSBAND THE BURDEN.
BECAUSE I WISH TO SPARE THE ENTIRE WORLD THE BURDEN.
IF THE SWORD IS INDEED CURSED, I WISH TO MASTER IT, AND THEREBY CALM THE CURSE.
I NEVER WANT IT TO HURT ANYBODY ELSE.

WHO TOLD YOU TO DO THIS?
PROFESSOR MASANOBU MIKAGE TOLD ME.
HE SAID THAT I MUST MASTER SWORDSMANSHIP SO THAT I MIGHT BECOME THE TRUE MASTER OF MURAMASA.
AND THAT I DON'T NEED TO KILL ANYONE, BUT MERELY FEED MURAMASA ON THE WIND.
KLINK
YES, THAT IS RIGHT. BUT YOU ARE FORGETTING A BASIC FACT.
SWORDS DISLIKE WOMEN.

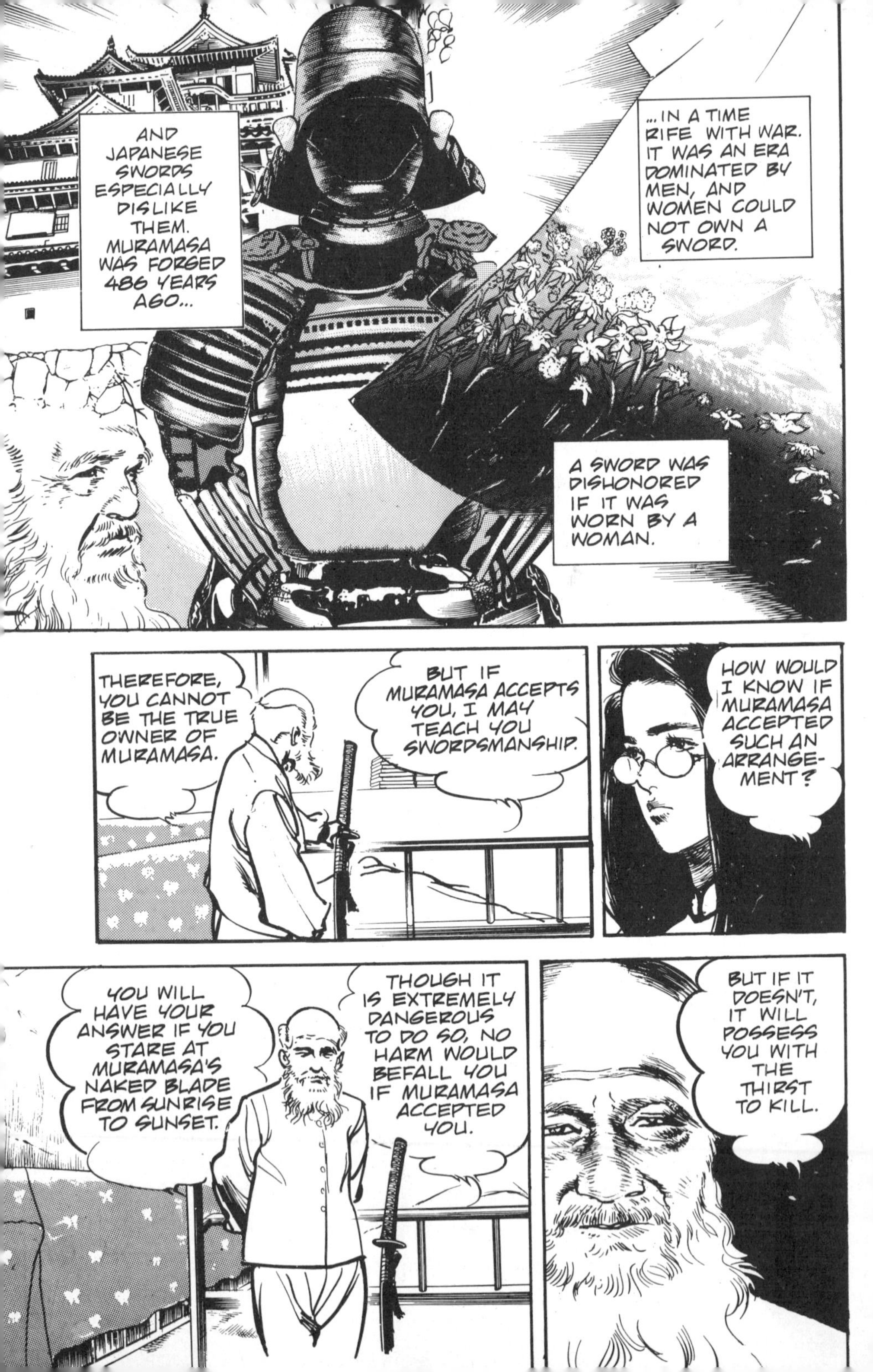

AND JAPANESE SWORDS ESPECIALLY DISLIKE THEM. MURAMASA WAS FORGED 486 YEARS AGO...

...IN A TIME RIFE WITH WAR. IT WAS AN ERA DOMINATED BY MEN, AND WOMEN COULD NOT OWN A SWORD.

A SWORD WAS DISHONORED IF IT WAS WORN BY A WOMAN.

THE WELL IS DRY AND DEEP, AND EVEN MURAMASA WILL NOT BE ABLE TO ESCAPE.
LET'S DROP MURAMASA INTO A WELL.
I WARN YOU. DON'T DO IT.

NO.
I WISH TO CALM THE SOUL IN THIS SWORD.

MMMM

HMMMM
PERHAPS MURAMASA HAS ALREADY POSSESSED YOU.

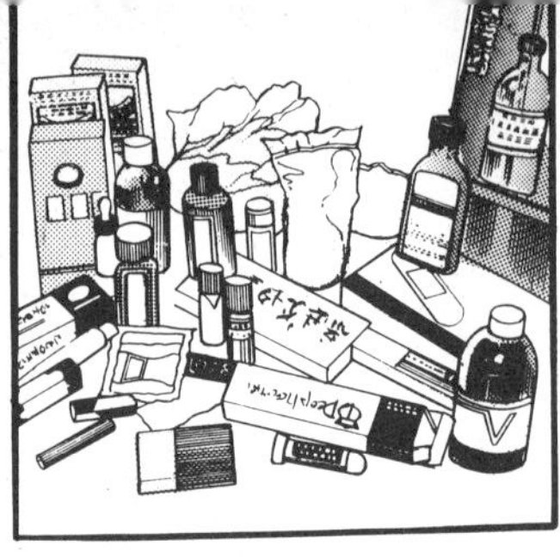

A DENTIST SHOULD HAVE SOME SORT OF SLEEPING PILLS AROUND.

CALMOTIN.

IT LOOKS SO OLD. I WONDER IF IT'S STILL POTENT.

GO AHEAD AND EAT. I DON'T HAVE MUCH, ONLY MY SPECIALTY.

PSSS

Ha ha ha ha ha ha.
AFTER ALL THAT TALK, IT WAS SO EASY TO TRICK HER. BUT IT'S BETTER THIS WAY.
I WILL THROW MURAMASA INTO THE WELL TOMORROW AT SUNRISE.
EVEN I DON'T WANT TO TOUCH IT NOW.

IT IS A DREADFUL SWORD.

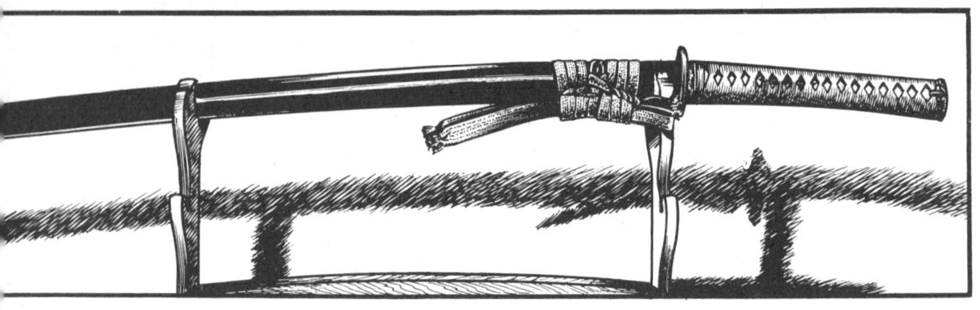

UGHHH

I WILL NEVER LET MY SISTER GO THROUGH WITH HER PLAN.
I WILL GET RID OF IT.

PLEASE, DON'T CURSE MY SISTER. CURSE ME INSTEAD.

Splitt
FLIP
FLIP
Ohhhh
Ahhhh
FLIP
EEE
EEE
KLINK

WHSSSH
WHSSSH
SLISH
phttt
WHSSSSSH
EEEE
EEEE
WHSSSH
WHSSSH

WHSSSH
WHSSSH
WHSSH

WHSSSH

Chapter 6 Sister Part 6

IVORY FAN!!

ARGGGH

IT'S ME, IVORY FAN. IT'S YOUR SISTER.

PLEASE, RETURN MURAMASA.

Thmmp

MMMMM

HMMM

WHOOOOOOOO

WHOOOOOO
KREEEK

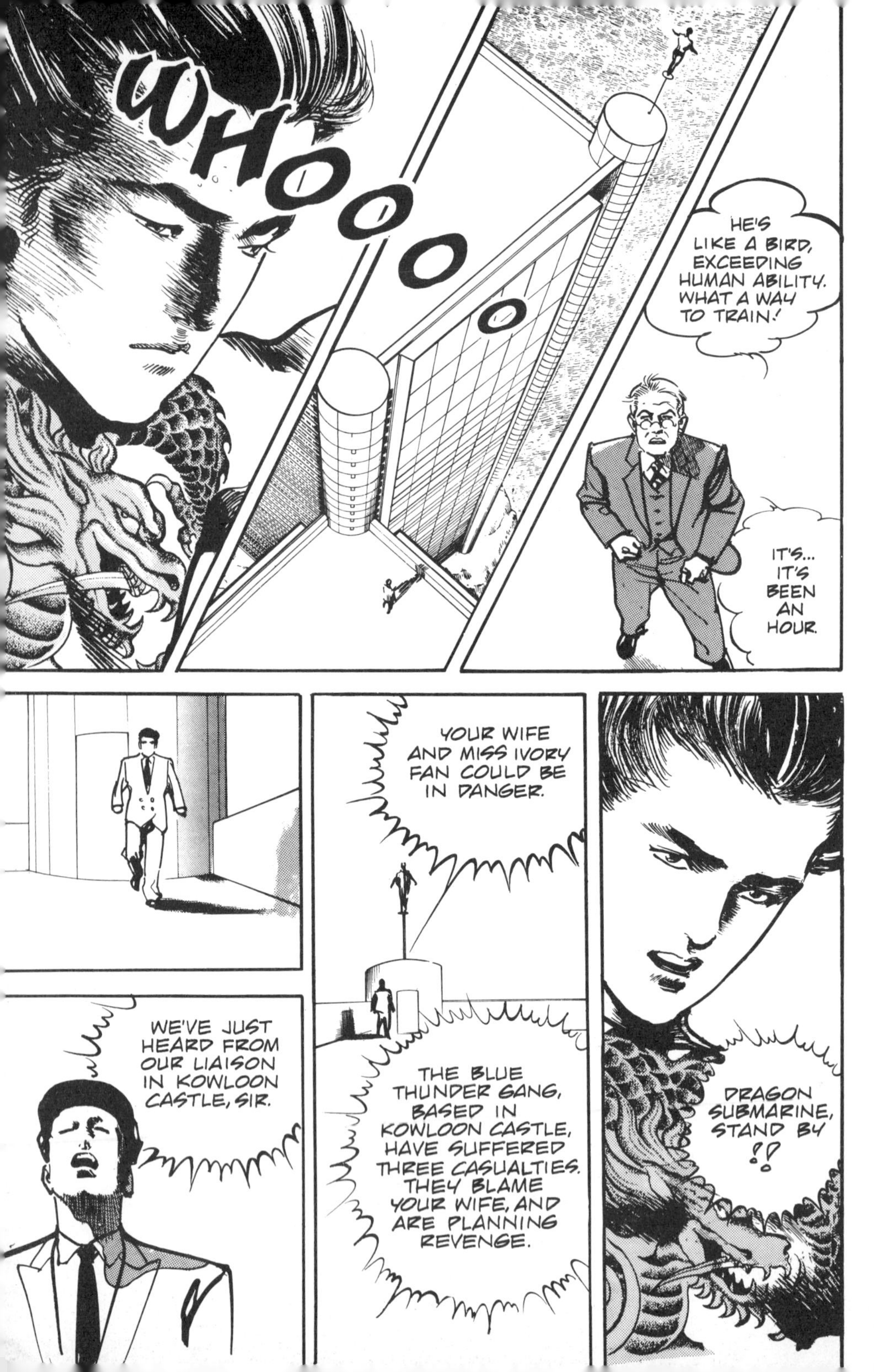

WHOOOOOO

HE'S LIKE A BIRD, EXCEEDING HUMAN ABILITY. WHAT A WAY TO TRAIN!

IT'S... IT'S BEEN AN HOUR.

AHHHHH
SPLSSH
PRRRRR

KLEE
KLEE

IT'S OKAY TO REST MURAMASA ON YOUR LAP IF YOU TIRE.

I WON'T GET TIRED.

HMMMM

DON'T YOU GET THE URGE TO ATTACK THE DOLL ?

NO. IT'S SUCH A SAD LOOKING DOLL. IT MAKES ME FEEL PITY.

HMMMM

Huh
?
ARRRRR!
I'LL HACK YOU TO PIECES FOR WHAT YOU DID TO OUR MEN!
FPPP

Sah!

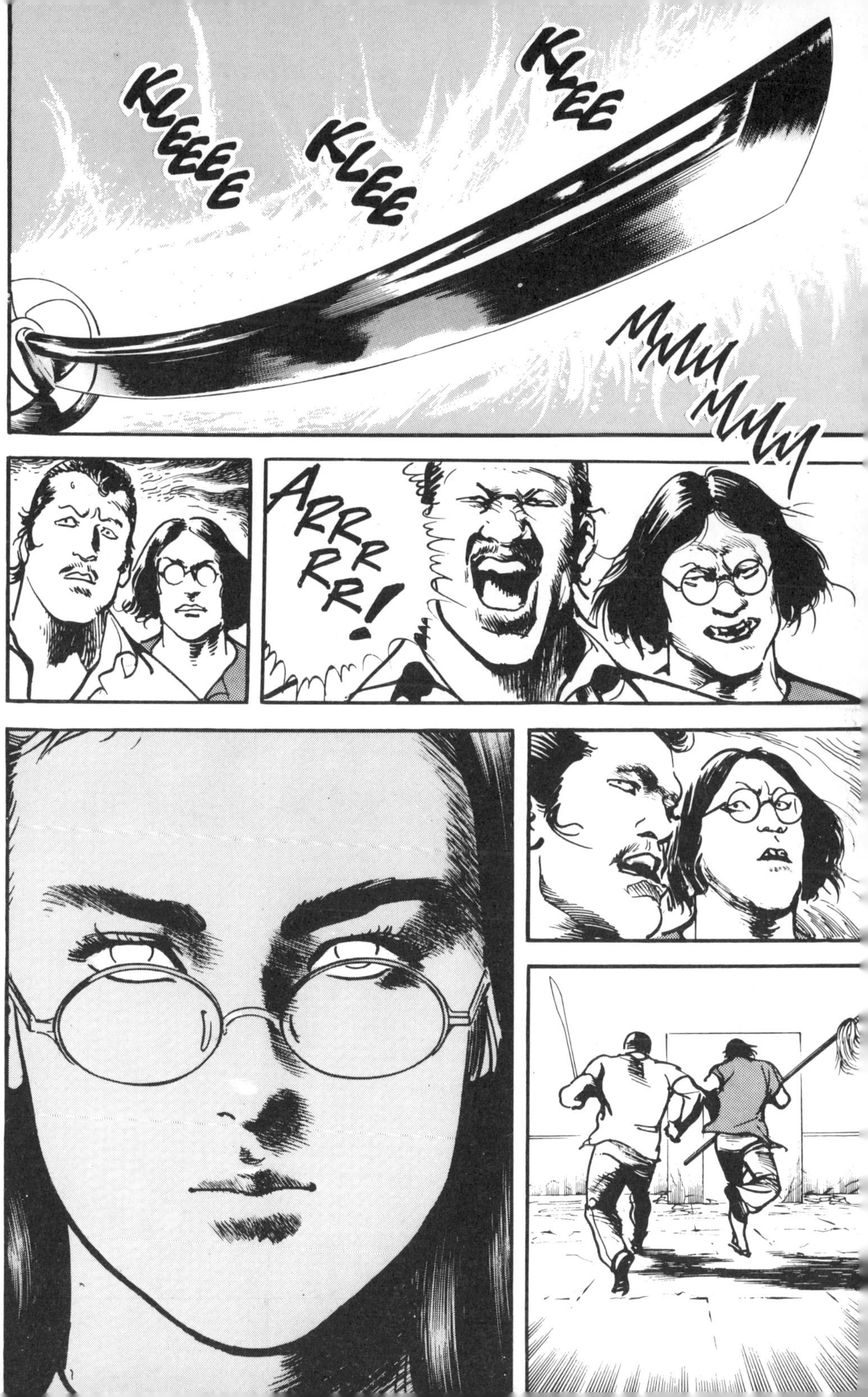

KLEEEEE
KLEEE
KLEEE
ARRRRRRR!

Ohhhh

INCREDIBLE, SISTER! YOU EVEN SCARED ME.

WHAT ?! ME? WHAT DID I DO ?

HOW STRANGE. BUT IT REALLY DID HAPPEN!!
MURAMASA MUST HAVE ACCEPTED YOU AS ITS TRUE OWNER.

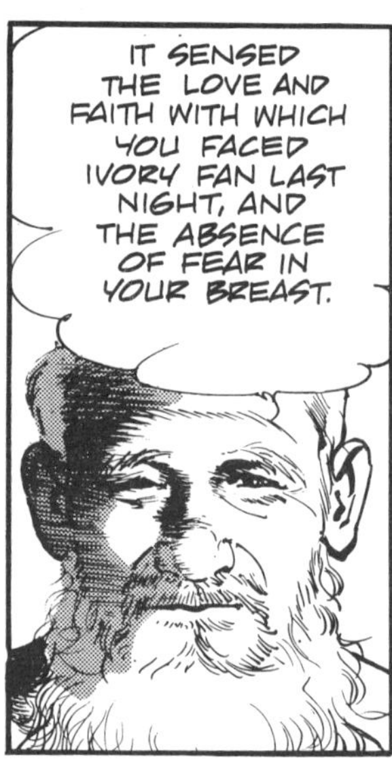
IT SENSED THE LOVE AND FAITH WITH WHICH YOU FACED IVORY FAN LAST NIGHT, AND THE ABSENCE OF FEAR IN YOUR BREAST.

I'M GLAD.

Chapter 6 Sister Part 7

TRP TRP

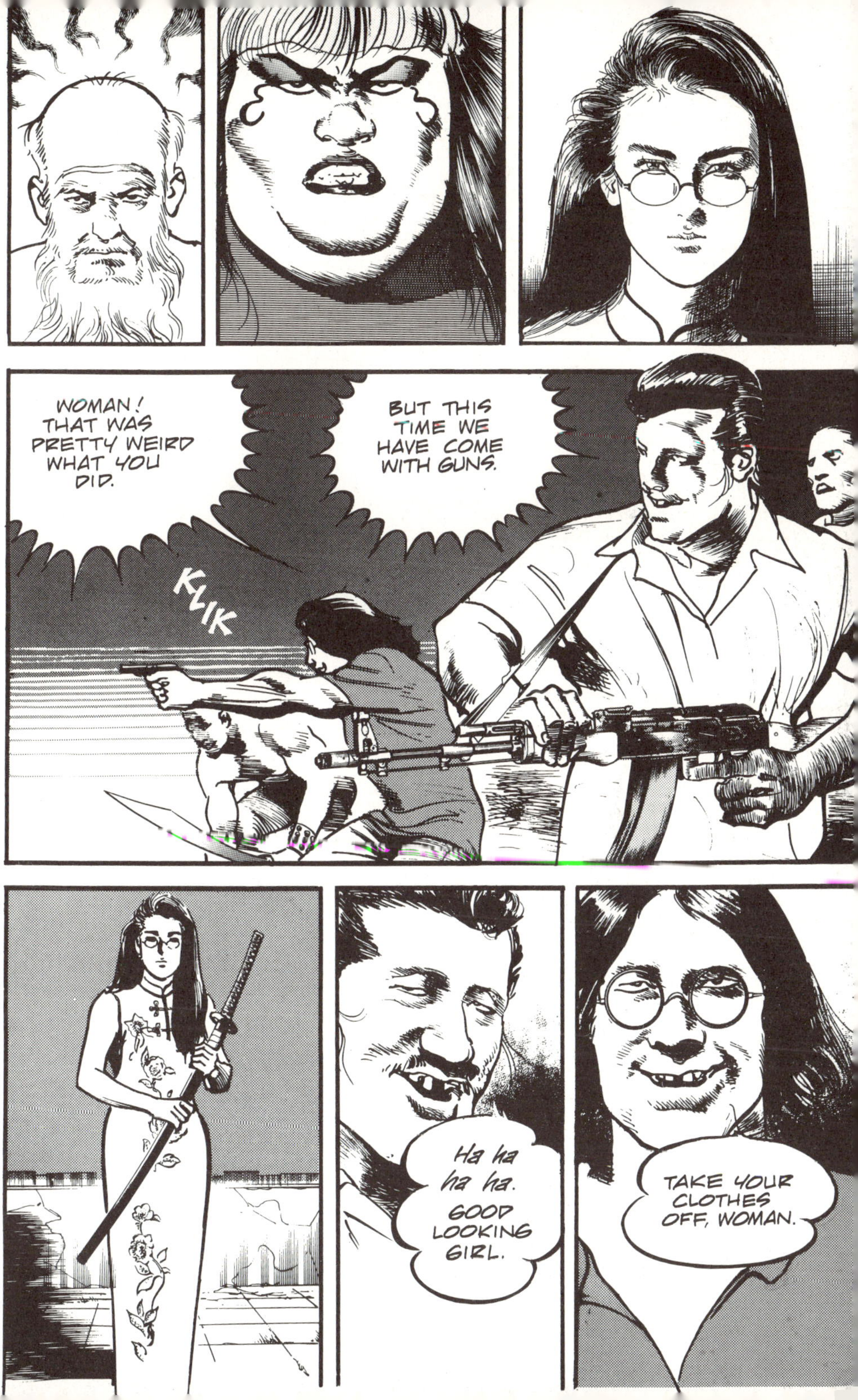

WOMAN! THAT WAS PRETTY WEIRD WHAT YOU DID.

BUT THIS TIME WE HAVE COME WITH GUNS.

KLIK

Ha ha ha. GOOD IDEA.
LET'S HAVE A LITTLE CHICKEN WITH OUR WINE!
YEAH, THERE'S A FULL MOON, TOO.
WHAT ARE YOU WAITING FOR? TAKE OFF YOUR CLOTHES. WE'LL SPARE YOUR LIFE IF YOU DO WHAT WE SAY.
ARGGGH
YAAAAA
BUDDA
BUDDA
TRTR
TRTR

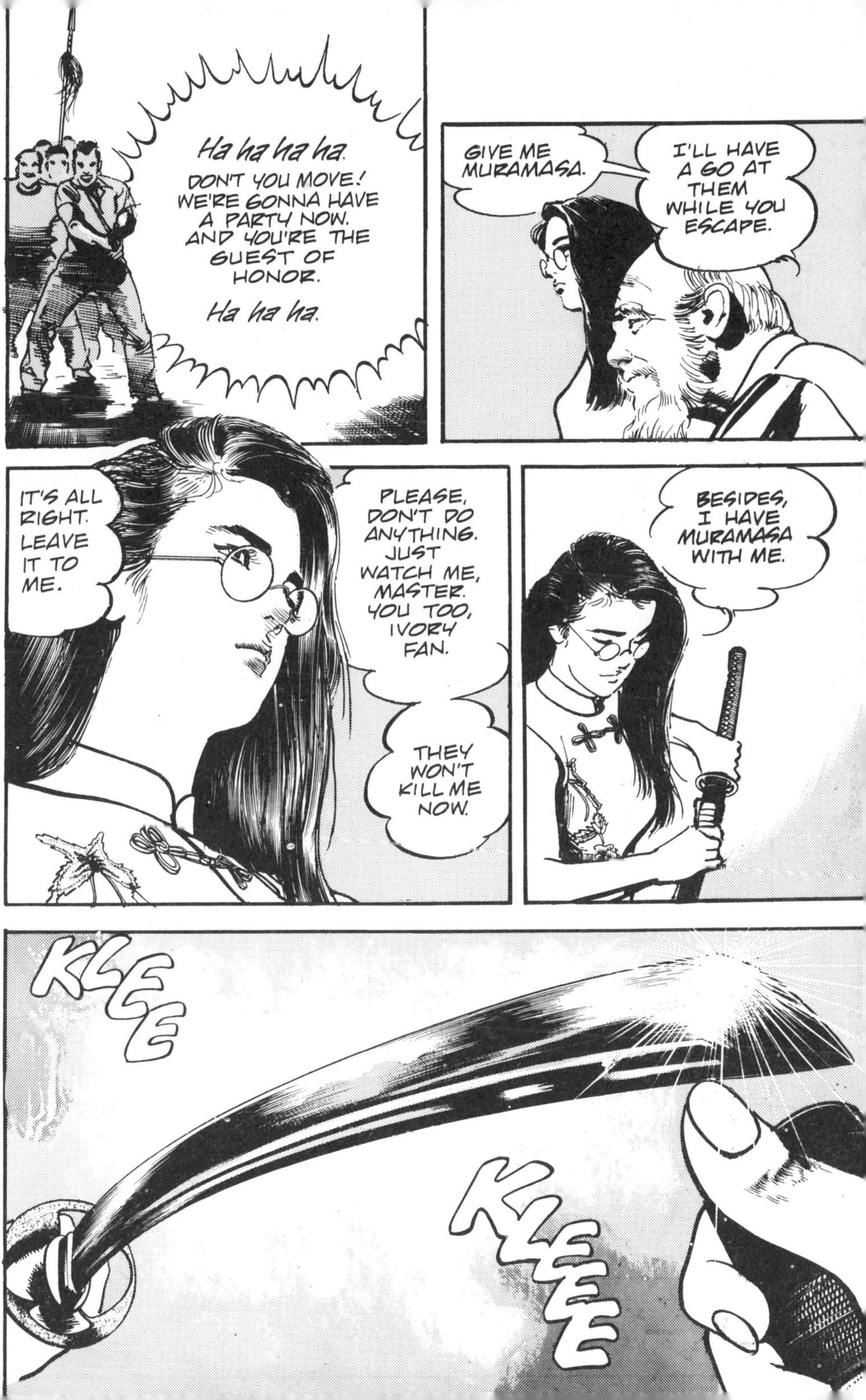

Ha ha ha ha.
DON'T YOU MOVE! WE'RE GONNA HAVE A PARTY NOW. AND YOU'RE THE GUEST OF HONOR.
Ha ha ha.

GIVE ME MURAMASA.

I'LL HAVE A GO AT THEM WHILE YOU ESCAPE.

IT'S ALL RIGHT. LEAVE IT TO ME.

PLEASE, DON'T DO ANYTHING. JUST WATCH ME, MASTER. YOU TOO, IVORY FAN.

THEY WON'T KILL ME NOW.

BESIDES, I HAVE MURAMASA WITH ME.

Huh?

KLIK

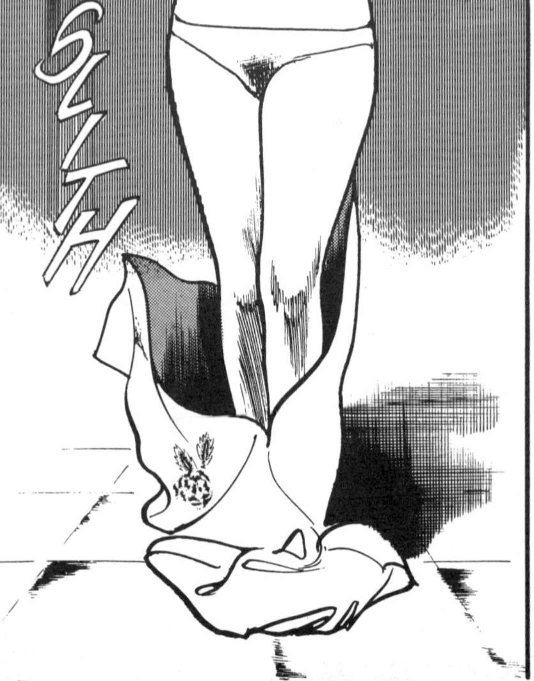

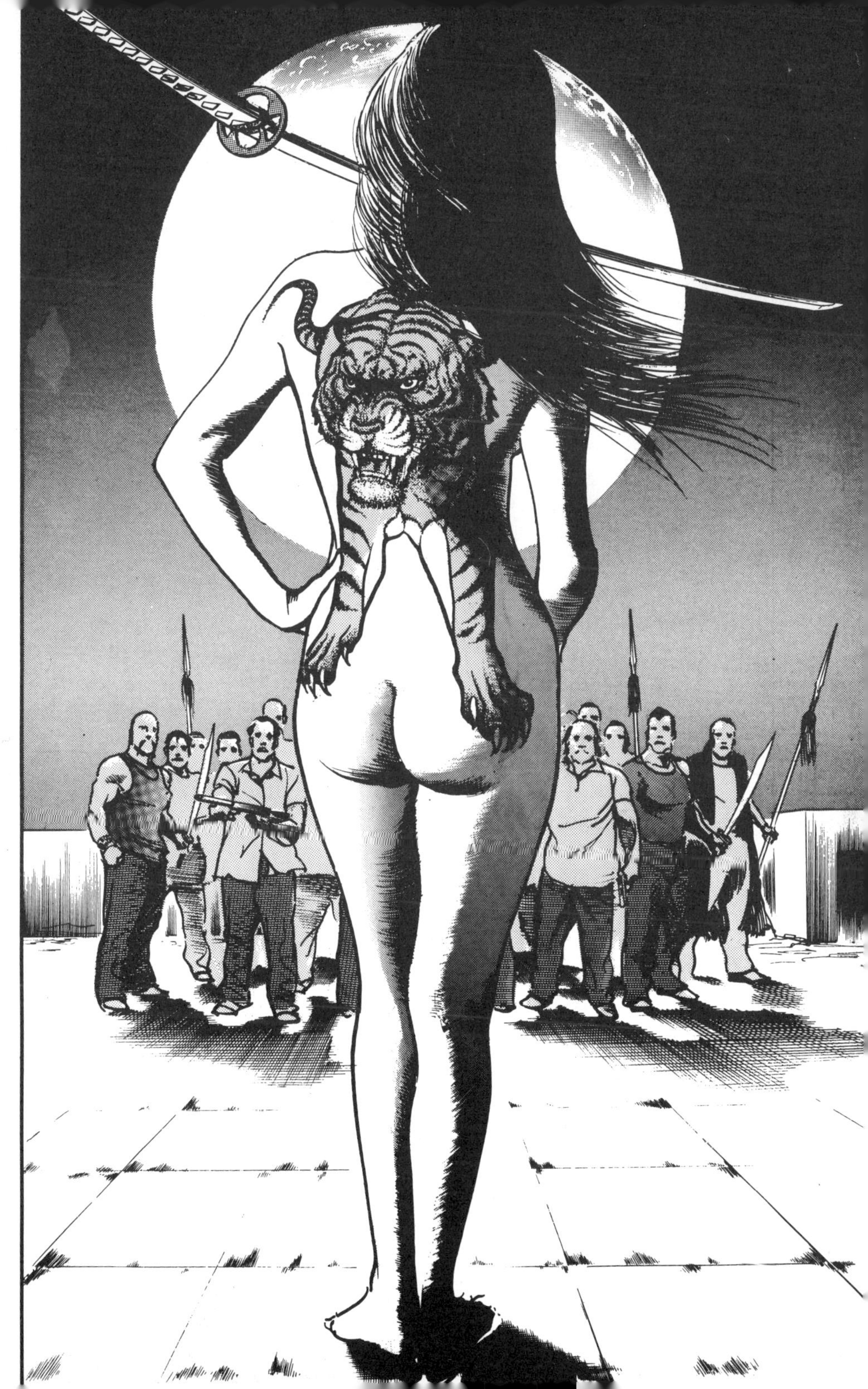

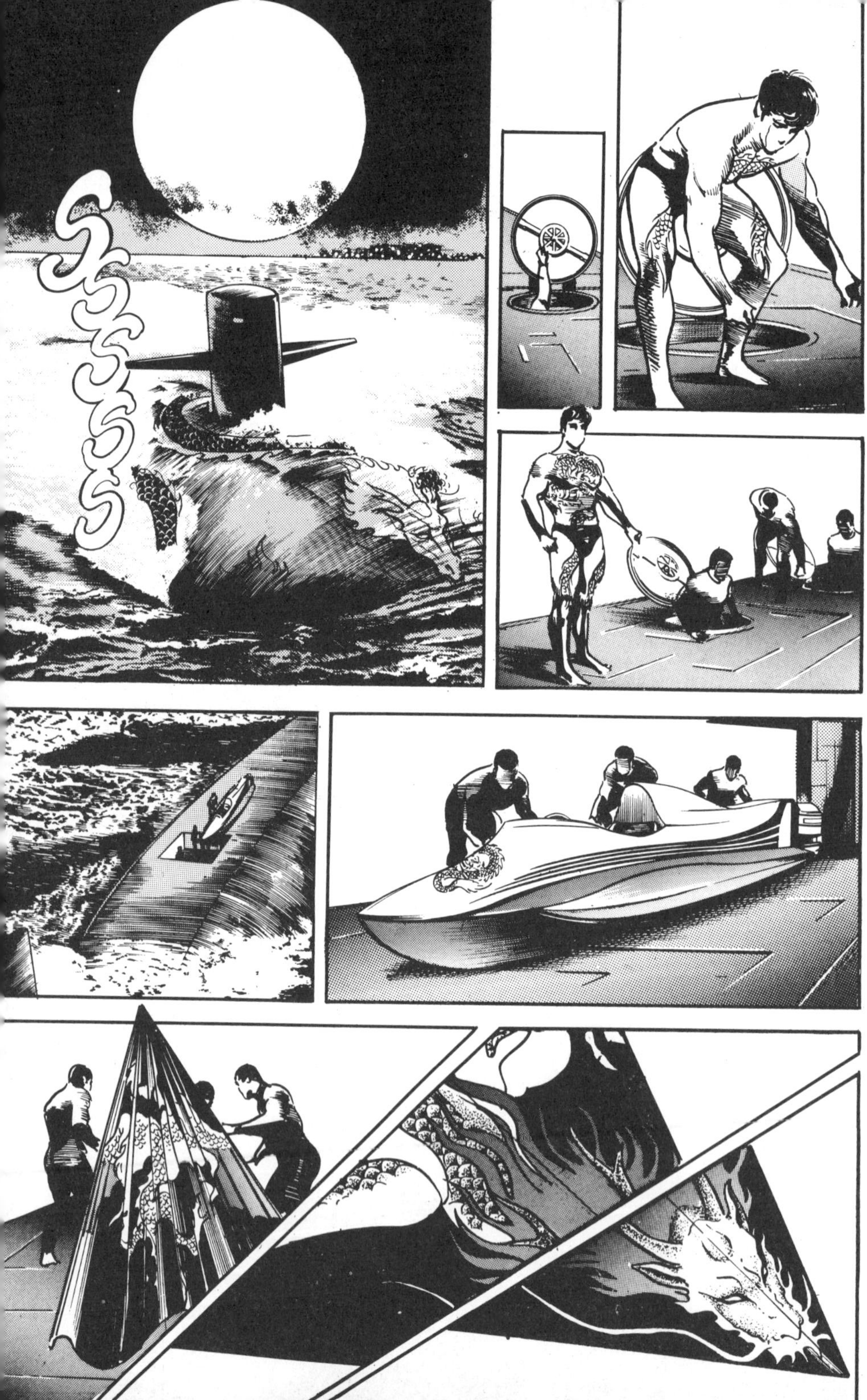
SSSSSS

QUICK
!

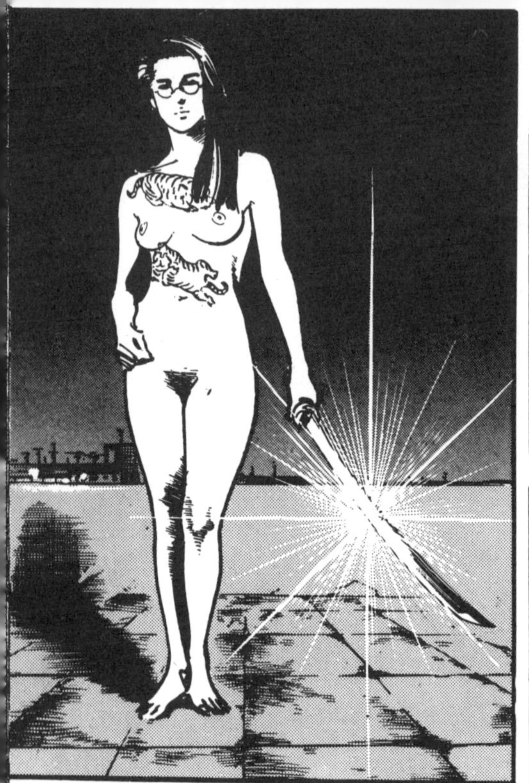

GOOD... REAL GOOD.

A NAKED WOMAN WITH A SWORD... WHAT A TURN-ON. DANCE, WOMAN. DANCE WITH YOUR FLASHING SWORD.

TAKE YOUR GLASSES OFF!

SISTER ?!?

DON'T WORRY.

MASTER, WOULD YOU MIND RECITING KAWANAKA-JIMA, THE SWORD DANCE ?

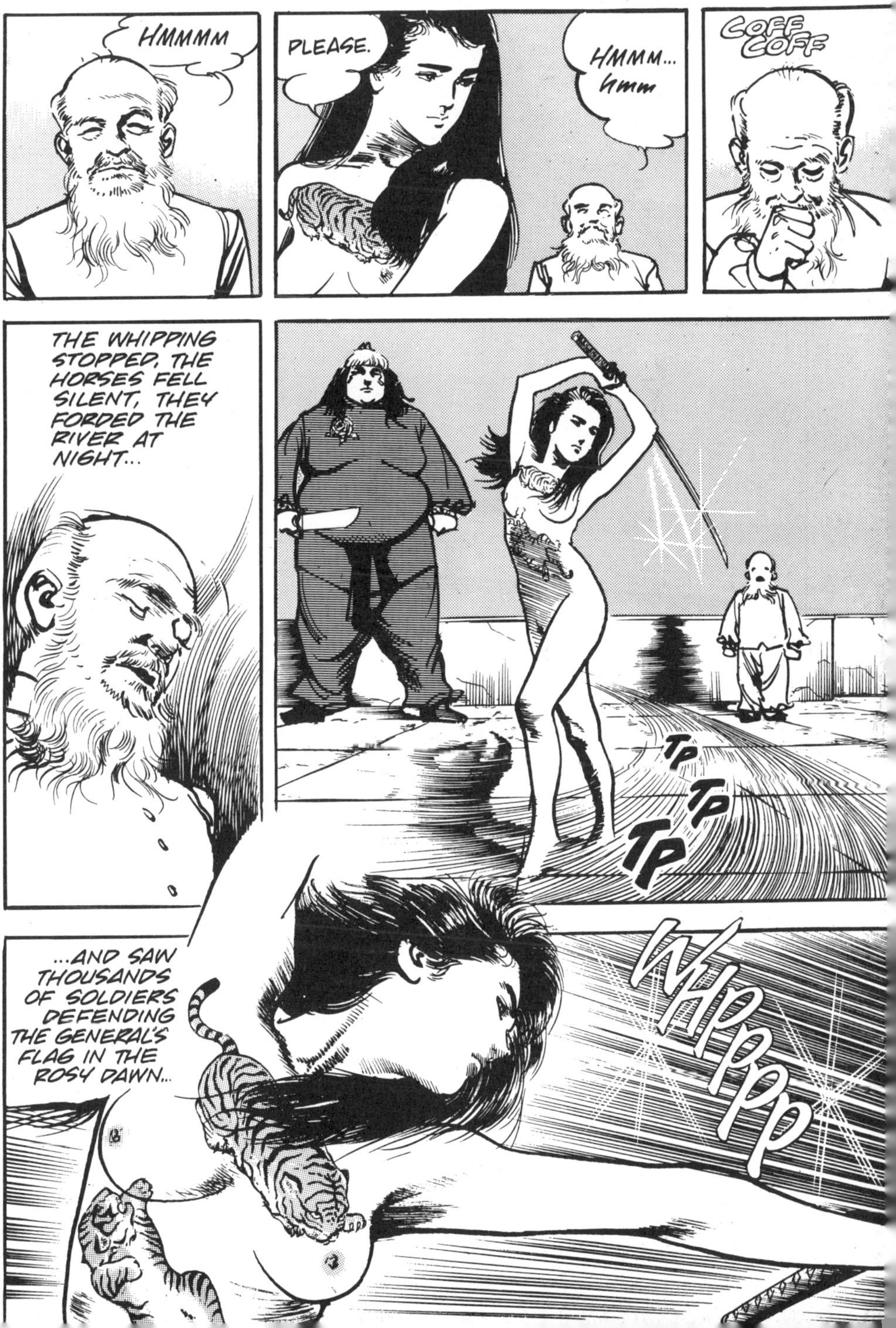

THE WHIPPING STOPPED, THE HORSES FELL SILENT, THEY FORDED THE RIVER AT NIGHT...

TP TP TP

...AND SAW THOUSANDS OF SOLDIERS DEFENDING THE GENERAL'S FLAG IN THE ROSY DAWN...

WHPPPP

YAAAAA
A GRUDGE HAD HONED HIS SWORDSMANSHIP FOR TEN YEARS...
WHP
WHP
WHP
MMMMM

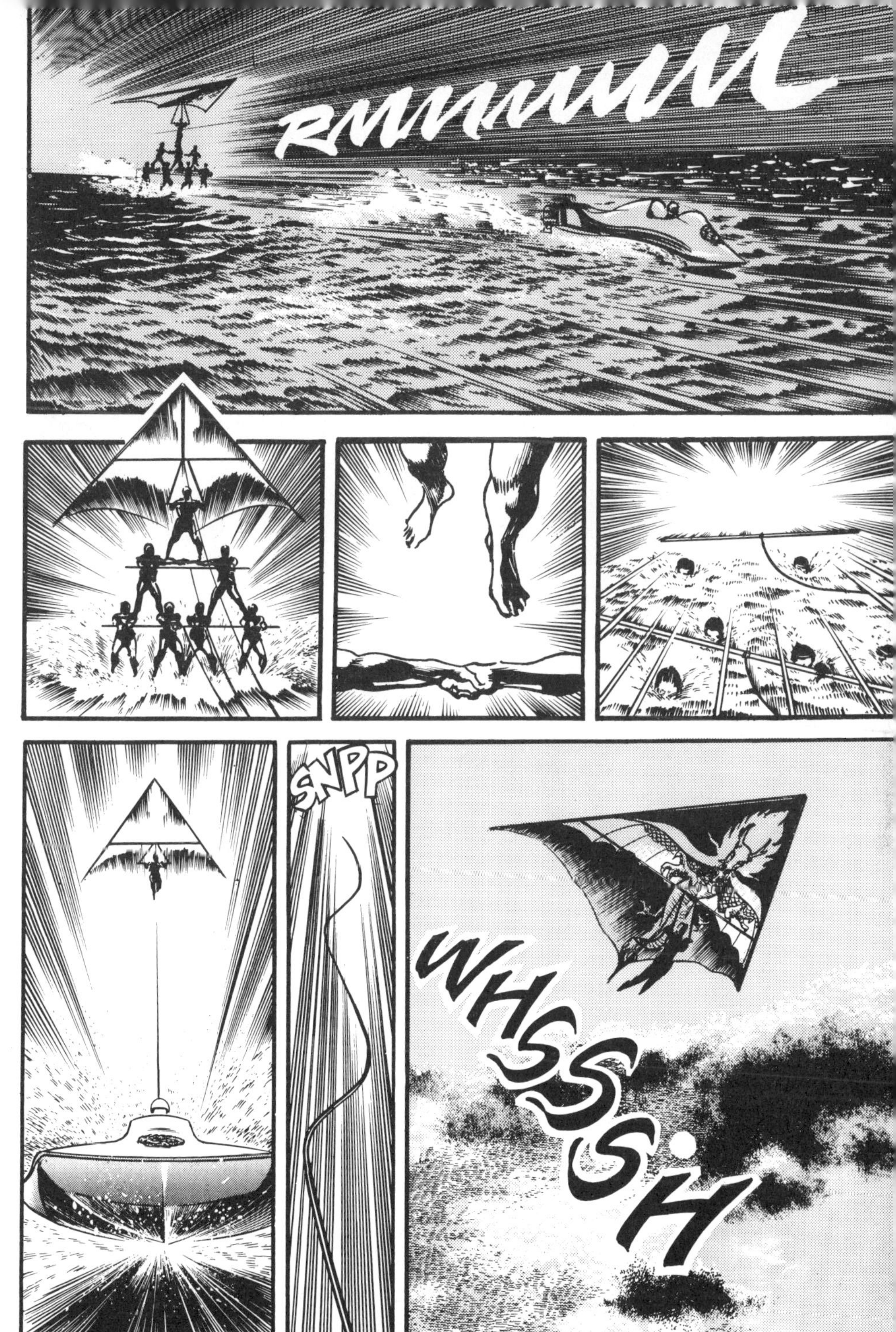
RMMMMM
SNPP
WHSSSH

...BUT SWINGING DOWN HIS FLASHING SWORD, HE HAD MISSED A GREAT OPPORTUNITY.

A DRAGON IS COMING!

HUH

THE TIGER SUMMONS THE DRAGON!
THE TIGER AND DRAGON SUMMON EACH OTHER!

WHSSH
WHSSH

WHA-?

D-D-
DEAR.

TP

ARE YOU ALL RIGHT ?
OF COURSE I AM.

END